THE THRESHOLD AND THE KEY

RYAN MADEJ

The Threshold and the Key © 2021 Ryan Madej

Originally Published by VoidFront Press, 2019

First Canadian Printing

ISBN: 978-1-7771304-4-2

Orbis Tertius Press

At a certain point I realized that the "I" doesn't exist. So I said to myself: If the "I" doesn't exist, I have to construct one, or maybe even more than one.

- Kathy Acker

Many a book is like a key to unknown chambers within the castle of one's own self.

- Franz Kafka

The Key to the language door is difficult to find, but once one steps over the Threshold all worlds open. There are many death traps, byways, tracks into the Unknown, and mysterious strangers along the way who have tried to stop my progress. No matter, they have been eradicated along with all the others. I was told to produce the Great Work, but in order to do it I had to be buried alive. I trapped myself with monsters and became lost in a dense fog and I think I've begun to find my way out of the burial chamber that lay at the bottom of the Trench: the soundless vacuum of the Sea, which nurtured and hindered my mind as the years passed into another kind of vacuum, that being the vacuum of Time and Space. The land-scape has changed; as a matter of fact, it has changed immensely without me noticing. Within a relatively short span of time the sky has turned grey, the river a deeper brown, and the once familiar places dens for ghosts. Memory, in all its fractured glory, is what remains. Let me piece it back together for you the way I always have with an unsteady hand and a clouded mind. Perhaps that is the real picture: the one written in the dead of night or during the intense heat of July as the fans move and spin. Regardless, the images and words spiral out like a pinwheel of madness upon the city . . .

*As this wave from memories flows in, the city soaks it up
like a sponge and expands.*

-Italo Calvino, Invisible Cities

So yes, the city sprang from the wellspring of
memories, fire, and subtle erotic gesture—a lens so
acute and clear that only now have I begun to *see*.
Of course, others were present too, for where
would I be without those other actors upon the
stage as the acts come to an end? All of this is
inescapable now, no matter what angle is taken or
road tread upon; as a matter of fact, the Wall
becomes higher and what lies beyond becomes
harder to see and contemplate. There is a solution,
however, hidden in the multitude of words.

One needs only to look at words like *mantra* or
hand to see what I'm getting at here: a way forward, a way out of the darkness and perhaps into
further darkness. The optimist will always believe
that the light is surely not that far ahead, while the
pessimist thinks it will never come back, whereas
the *realist* accepts the possibility that the light
doesn't exist at all. This was, and continues to be,
the reality of Midtown and the citizens that dwell
within its walls, including myself; a city bereft of
an identity or much of anything else for that
matter. Empty cafés and restaurants, lonely back
alleys, the Bridge of Suicides, and the sounds of

the orgasmic spectacle reverberating throughout the dusty, uneven streets. This is the path I chose for myself, or rather the prison I chose for myself: the Library, the Flesh, the Smoke, the Unknown. All these Elements serve as a way forward, or at least they did at one time or another and got me to the place in which I now reside. In a time of strange polarities, floods and torture becoming everyday rituals and events, or where executions and Ebola drift and pulse everywhere, my existence takes on a whole new meaning. A fanatical warped ride out into passwords and spyware. I don't fret though because I hold the Key and I've already stepped over the Threshold . . .

The last journey of the flâneur: death. Its destination: the New. Deep in the unknown to find the New.

-Walter Benjamin

Someone once asked me: What are the conditions of insanity? Or rather, what are the conditions of *sanity*??? A question not easily answered, but a question worth the effort. The growth of my own sanity must have begun early, before my departure from the Vayu* and on the backstreets between the Western Quarter and the deep recesses of the Square. Who really knew a city well? Joyce, Borges, Dostoyevsky, etc. All burdened by the magnificence and history, the squalor and strangeness of the City, whose majesty is the stories created within its limits and told to the world. Yes, I began to create my own story, my own perception of these walls and streets that bound me and found their way onto the page, sometimes in torrents but often in dribbles and random fragments. To quote Benjamin again: "Significant literary work can only come into being in a strict alternation between action and writing." Correct, so very correct, but one can also say: "The significant city can only come into being in a strict alternation between its citizens and its geography." As the horizon changes, so too does the citizen and vice versa, leaving both in a state of perpetual change and hopeful evolution. Bastion Perrot's hope when he founded the city so long ago along with his three acolytes in tow from the Continent was to bring the charm and mystery of the esoteric with them in order to build something fantastic and lasting. Within a generation, as was told in the Marble Corridor* and other junctures, a grey pall came with them and never really left.

. . . And from their own personal languages came the Four Districts, each representing one of the Elements of Air, Earth, Water, and Fire. Not surprisingly, each one of them under the belief that the Universe somehow destined them for the task of founding a city, realized that their astrological Sun signs aligned with the four cardinal signs of the Zodiac: Libra, Capricorn, Cancer and Aries, thus sparking a creative surge which one finds engraved on the various monuments and key points in each of the districts. The common citizen is unaware of most of these symbols and mani-festations and it would serve them well to study what is around them, but that may be a lost cause.

Regardless, as my vision cleared or at least became *attuned* to this new language, my mind began to reel and change. As I said goodbye to the Vayu I couldn't help but cry internally at what I was about to lose and it would be many moons and sunrises before I would return and realize that what brought me the most comfort had been lost to the ravages of time and progress. No matter, I guess, that is the way of things and the way of cities great and small, but the way forward is also the way back. So again: What are the conditions of sanity? Finding the way back to yourself, no doubt . . . Some way through all the cities*. So let the rest of the story be told through the following:

The Threshold, the Key, the Library, the Flesh, the Smoke, and the Unknown until we arrive back in the swirling dark Sea of the Trench where it all began and this, too, will End.

The Library: it never allows you a complete return to the world you once knew; as a matter of fact, it may even *replace* the world you once knew, making that so-called imaginary world the basis for major decisions in one's life. I can say this is true from experience and that the naiveté of the impressionable young reader can make for strange experiences. During my teen years I discovered the Beat writers and like any teenager whose only sense of rebellion came through the books he read, the Beats were an ideal choice. They were cool, intelligent, and also dared to seek the Unknown, but none so much as William S. Burroughs: El Hombre Invisible. Burroughs recounts his early admiration of writers and their lives full of adventure, drugs, and insight and wanting to be just like them. Of course, anyone who is familiar with *The Naked Lunch*, *The Soft Machine*, or *The Wild Boys*, knows that he took what he supposed a writer should be to the nth degree, which translated into a bohemian, narcotic fuelled landscape where the Word became the enemy . . .

He wasn't wrong. The Word, even if we can become friends with it, is still essentially the enemy of progress when it comes to writing, as contradictory as that sounds. The symbolic on the other hand, which Burroughs was also interested in through Mayan and Egyptian hieroglyphs, paints a far more powerful picture of the human experience than ordinary words do. The Cut-Up that Burroughs employed in many of his works was a way of cutting through the Word, perhaps in an effort to discover the *esoteric aspects of language*. As a reader of his books, at the time I felt somewhat alienated from the world he created, but it also felt very alive and familiar to me in ways I could not and still cannot explain.

So yes, in a way literature began to *replace* my reality and the more I read, the more I lost touch with what was real. Copious amounts of marijuana didn't help the situation, but it didn't necessarily hinder it either because that crossing over into the realm of the Library and Smoke, dreams and fragments, began to change my thought patterns in such a way that replacing my idea of reality was really more of an *opening* of reality. To look at Burroughs, or someone like Joyce who took language to extremes in *Finnegans Wake*, one can look at certain kinds of writing as *mantras** that burrow beneath the surface of consciousness and awaken something primal and meaningful to the rare individual. Maybe the best writing is what does this: gets us closer to the deeper levels of our collective consciousness where we begin to understand the symbolic. One need only to look at the ideas behind the Kabbalah or Tibetan mysticism to see the connection.

This didn't happen with me, or at least not in the beginning. One can go years after reading specific books and never understand their true value until one day an outer experience, separate from the story, illuminates the words. I had such experiences once the substance of choice changed from the aroma of the herb to the dryness of the mushroom. Now, the 'revelations' surrounding psychedelics are varied and often overlapping, but I can say with ease that once I began using psilocybin that perhaps is when the Threshold I imagined since my first days in the Vayu came into view, though distant and blurry. I've commented on synchronicity before and the Nexus* that followed, but perhaps I didn't elaborate on how the two were connected. Within a year the *intensity and volume* of the events were occurring at such a rate that I seriously began to question my sanity. You've heard this story before, haven't you? And again, the old sanity question . . . What are the conditions of the sane?

The candle was certainly lit and the image I saw in the mirror had begun to shift.

Perhaps this is where the villainy emerges from all of this in the subtlest of ways. A way *forward,* or rather, a sharper way *inward.* The knife has to pierce the skin, so to speak; but in this case the blade needs to be run down the middle of one's personality and then we have to wait to see what spills out at the end. The awful stench of what emerges can be unsettling, and (of course) what then? One may ask themselves this question over and over and never come to a definitive conclusion, but the fact remains that the entrails of one's being are still lying on the floor . . .

What I felt growing from the putrid mess I had

created by my own self-dissection can only be described as *liberation*; a liberation from all that I had told myself to be true in my youth. But let me be clear on one point: this never felt conscious or contrived, but rather a natural progression toward a goal I had only glimpsed through the lens of literature and the like. Even if I wasn't a villain in the conventional sense of the word, I certainly began feeling like a villain to myself and that became frightening.

The cold drew itself in as I stepped over the Threshold and I tried to focus my eyes beyond the cloud of blue smoke before me, fearing the dreary icicles of death beyond its vapours, like any good boy would at that age (13?). This was not the first time and it certainly wouldn't be the last. He had just left, I thought . . . Friday night . . . early spring dampness in the air . . . the call of erotic promises and spaces hidden from view. I opened the window in my room and breathed in the ozone, staring blankly at the sun setting in the West. Two long days alone, drifting in and out of a house that lay mainly dormant throughout the cool sleepless nights and dewy mornings, trying to make sense out of the senseless. She had left a few months before . . . the maternal figure . . . but every so often she would appear like a spectre, a tired and angry look on her face as if to say *where is he now?* *have you eaten?* etc. . . . Despite her anger and concern for my well-being, I secretly showed little aversion to being alone. Once my belly was full and the door was locked once more I was free. I spent long periods by the window deep into the night, wondering where he might be, and then as sleep found its way into my bones again I slipped under a blanket in the living room and pulled it over my head hoping, usually in vain, he would be there when I opened my eyes in the morning.

THE THRESHOLD AND THE KEY

My eyes had begun to fail. Cold, antique shadows drifted over my empty glass that was copper coloured and burnt green. My stride had become shorter and all I wanted to do was drink coffee and greet the frost of the coming winter. Reading my horrorscope was a terrible idea as it always seems to be in the End; it forbade me to go into the City alone, but I was already in the City and I was already alone. No footsteps down the hallway, only silence, and a deep white fog flowing in over the marble steps that led to the garden. It is there in the Western Quarter* that I buried my life, the life I wanted, and the life I needed. All the actors from the play that was my former life have exited stage left. Now I just fan the candle flame that is about to burn out completely. I throw cold water on my face and dream of inhaling and exhaling the aroma of fresh flowers. Dwelling in the sun as a child, the thought of the coming winter made no sound inside my head . . . Now it is all I can think about, as barbarous and colourless as that can be at times. The synthetic city has held me in its arms for too long, all perfumed and powdered. Showers of rain and Hanged Men in parkades. Lilacs and clairvoyants and the suicides of the High Gate Bridge*. A City of the Dead, so to speak, or to put it another way entirely by Calvino: "Cities, like dreams, are made of desires and fears, even if the thread of their discourse is secret, their rules are absurd, their perspectives deceitful, and everything conceals something else." And yes, Midtown has always concealed something else. This all goes back to the founder himself, Bastion Perrot, who, on the hunt for the Stone of the Philosophers, felt the desire to create it in the form of this city that sits on the Plains . . .

Some might say that all the beauty Midtown once had can be attributed to his wife: Madelaine de Garza, the Portuguese occultist who was his true initiator into the magickal arts. Not only was she a dreamy beauty from Lisbon, but she was also privy to all types of knowledge surrounding architecture, perhaps because of her lineage—her father was rumoured to be a 33rd Degree Mason. Perhaps it was through the Craft that she learned the ways of encoding secrets in stone, or in bas-reliefs, or in the monuments that are scattered around Midtown. Of course, due to the legends and the byways of time, a sense of what may be true or false is of course a matter of belief or non-belief. Despite this, her spirit, as it was described in the various histories of Midtown, was one of lightness and colour amongst the citizens she encountered and interacted with and heavy or introspective within the tight circle that was the three other Founders. Bastion described her in a diary discovered after his death as "the vital and vibrant energy that binds this city together and binds my heart to hers."

Lovely words for a lovely lady, I suppose. Amidst all the correspondence and personal letters of the Master Bastion she's mentioned no less than 400 times, and it would seem with the utmost affection and reverence. A love story so complete that maybe even Shakespeare himself would be jealous. Perhaps the only tragedy that seemed to befall their relationship was the fact that they were never able to have children. This feeling was reflected in de Garza's own diaries, which lay protected under glass in the large esoteric wing of the Old Library near the centre of Midtown. Dated October 15th 1844, she says:

"The punishment of God is not complete until a woman like myself, so many leagues away from the Creator in thought and body, is given over to barrenness and unable to conceive a child even after desiring it more than anything in this world. When I look into the eyes of the one I love I can see the same sadness and sorrow I carry within me, yet within him it is something more of a defeat . . . Perhaps all that can be done is the Great Work itself . . . the binding of Sun and Moon within the bricks of this city. But there is more than just us, there are the other two as well: Overbeck and Junichiro, who dared just as much as we did to create something fruitful and grand, though isn't creating a child the most daring act of all? Bastion might agree with me on this point but I seem to see less of him these days. Why, I ask myself? Does he not cling to me as we sleep in our chamber together, his arm around my waist and his lips on my neck? Perhaps he wants this child more than me, but that is hard to imagine. What he imagines is something bigger and brighter than both of us, something that will outlast a hundred generations, like the Pyramids. Have we accomplished that here in this city?

How will we ever know? Bastion, it would seem, has a feeling that we will live forever . . . my empty womb tells me differently."

Yes, that was de Garza in her own words, a woman whose words lie under glass only to be looked at and not drawn upon. Someone in need of refreshment could slake their thirst with her wisdom, but who knows the tale of her or even of this city? No one but myself, I suppose. A wanderer like herself and Bastion and the rest.

Madelaine and her womanly haze under sultry light and electric heat, hypnotized and keeper of the silent motto which is Time and Death, leaping through fields of thought and milking the constellations. Empty and silent is the city that the Four built, but that's the way that I like it . . . or do I? Or is it that I have yet to discover all its secrets, all its shadows, and all its crimes? Out of Order comes Chaos, the quantum versus the relative, the push and pull of the Four Forces of Nature. Bastion felt dignified in the flames of the White Salamander, spreading the ashes of bones in the Circle . . .

THE THRESHOLD AND THE KEY

He kept time with the Seasons and held the Wind in his belly to feed the heat. Shuttered and removed from the whir and clang of the outside world he attained something higher and greater. That was the essence of the ritual of the White Salamander. Eating and dancing, living within the seasonal blisses and creating a new sacrament around the bonfire, breaking open the Old and building the New.

(N-27 $\triangle$ 5 trident 3-8 (greater than the negative) O times O times P) the Tao $\triangle$ epsilon squared

THE MEEK INHERIT NOTHING

So, what do you do? Take a gamble, leg it across no man's land and hope for the best? (The man does sound desperate.) Or take time to assess the situation, then devise a plan that's effective and safe? ~~What would you do in a situation like this?~~ Officers are taught on training exercises like this that there's no room for pointless heroics in the Army. ~~Take a gamble, leg it across no man's land and hope~~ Could you make a calm, rational decisions in the most emotional situations? ~~Or take time to assess the situation, then devise a plan that's~~ If you're aged 16-24, ideally with A-levels or a degree, call 0345 300 111 (quote ref. 2909) or write to AOE, Freepost 4335, Dept 2909, Bristol BS1 3YX.http://www.army.mod.uk The Army is committed to being an Equal Opportunities Employer.

BURIED ALIVE

Paranoid complication

The record pops and hisses on the turntable and the television is blaring. Walking into the living room, I see him passed out on the floor in a pile of vomit. I turn off the turntable and television and he stirs from the floor after I shake him a little . . . *Wake up, what's going on?* He opens his eyes, somewhat stunned he is on the floor and perhaps even more surprised he got sick as well. Standing up, he quickly falls backwards into the plant by the window, nearly knocking it down. His image smolders in the mirror and he looks pale from the drink, as well as from the midwinter depression that seems to run in the family. I know why he has done this: the Maternal Figure is out of town, out of reach, and certainly out of his immediate thoughts. He slinks off to the bathroom to scrub the area rug of vomit while I stand before the living room mirror and wonder if I'll be like him one day. It is only now, decades later, that the seeds of those strange evenings come to bear fruit. The scene shifts. A thousand zeroes and ones falling from the skies in crazy technicolor. Only nickels left in my pockets, all the quarters are gone. Across the Square two chess players are hunched over the board . . . King and Queen . . . Midsummer death throes and the ever maddening wind picking up from the north. I drink a cherry cola and sit and watch the jazz ensemble, wishing deep down for a puff of an Old Port or a sweet Javanese cigar. An attractive girl walks by: part mad-hatter, part mad poet. I see her scribbling haikus in a notepad after she sits down, hand and eyes blazing in a deep manna of plasma or pleasure, I don't know which, really. I have a strange desire to strip her of the noise and awful smells of the Square and drink coffee or tea with her and maybe splatter a little blood. I do nothing instead and continue listening to the music. The trio is playing Coltrane's *Moment's Notice*. Why am I sitting here in the first place? He never did show like he was supposed to. Typical. Like some sort of ghost of memory whose face seems vague in my mind's eye from time to time, even as I squint hard to remember the good times past. I turn to the girl, now many verses into her masterwork, and I smile . . .

Clothes on for now, I moved toward her slowly but carefully. From the semi-hidden picture I had seen, she looked like a bit of a freak in the sheets. This was a scene like all the other scenes: sordid but ultimately satisfying. I arrived snow-blind and juvenile, but by the end felt like a newly focused individual. She quietly answered the door. Shorter than I expected, red-haired. A bad dye job. Vague smell of fat and perfume in the air, a strange contrast to her flawless young body that looked so smooth in early winter glare. We undressed and I looked at her for a moment, catching an ounce of fragility and innocence in her face. In comparison, I had lost mine long ago, or at least it seemed that way as I took one last glance at myself in the mirror before we laid down on the bed underneath a black tinted light. I felt as though I had cheated death for some reason as I placed my mouth over her clitoris. Bygone days and black rainbows flooded my mind as my tongue searched her vagina for the answer to a question I couldn't remember asking myself. Maybe because I thought this was the true beginning of something. I asked her to turn over so I could take her from behind . . . Sorcery in full swing, full erection and come in a blinding wail of pleasure . . . Alpha graced you and fucked you.

. . . And somewhere beyond the sphere of decency, good taste, and respectability, I lost myself amongst the flesh of Others. She sucked with exuberance, pleasantly but forcefully, my hand on her silken hair. I freely cupped her breast in my palm, smiling a strange smile as I looked at the ceiling, my semen exploding in the condom. She lifted her head, half invisible in the dark . . . *Was it good, babe?* I said nothing and tossed the condom in the wastebasket and squeezed her breast one more time for good measure. She turned from the window and snickered at me . . . *You have an extra cigarette?* I placed the cigarette in her hand and she leaned in and kissed my mouth. *We should see each other again sometime, don't you think?* Nodding in agreement, I unlocked the door and she made her way out. She gave me another kiss and I could taste the mixture of tobacco and lemon candy on her breath. She walked back toward Salamander Road, occasionally looking over her shoulder to see if I was still there and I gave her a tiny wave. My penis was flaccid and worthless again, but in good spirits. My mind drove off and I heard a few days later that her throat was slit, or at least that is what the locals told me. That her body was found in the river valley near the Velox, not far from the High Gate Bridge, actually. We were strangers but a chill went through my body, not because of the bloody way in which she died, but because she no longer existed at all. A pawn removed off the chessboard of life. It happened in early May if I recall correctly, which is to say I may be wrong, yet I sense the smell of lilac and lavender in the air and the sound of birds in the early morning. To die at the height of spring before the damning heat of the coming summer is perhaps one of the few gifts one can ask for . . . right?

The Story of L.

Passing under the streetlamps in the dead of night brings forth the madness of memory, doesn't it? Regret is a funny word and not one used lightly, simply because I don't have many regrets even if the demons of past memories rear their ugly heads and dance upon the present. However, this one may be listed under regret, or maybe even despair; a rare kind of despair that trickles through the years and eats you from the inside. Who was L. anyway? I wish I knew, or at least knew more. She appeared quite out of nowhere, through a veil of mist and shadow, smoking a cigarette across the parkade and waving to me as I too inhaled the smoke of death and savoured its touch upon my lungs. We worked in the same sphere of dullness and disorder, rants and rages, and the uncertainty of the new century. The course by which we moved toward each other — or rather, away from each other — is really the basis of my regret and one of the reasons I can no longer cry over the loss of Flesh.

Perhaps in some remote Unknown way she was the catalyst for what became the Nexus; that large, looming phenomenon that became my unravelling only a couple years after her appearance. To say I became depressed and despondent is only a byproduct of something more sinister and erotic that lay with her. She became the embodiment of my world at a particular moment in time, even though nothing physical occurred between us . . . Yet, the *potential* was more than obvious. So obvious in fact that the *potential* could have easily become *kinetic* . . .

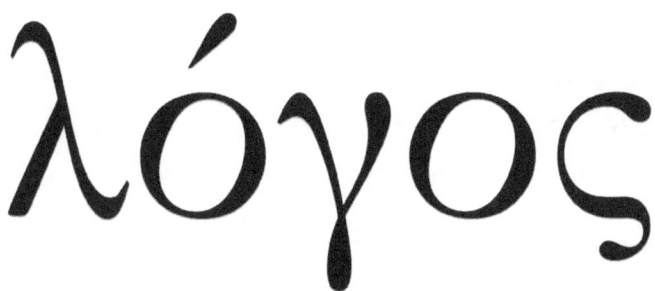

She often spoke of dream sequences that I would appear in with her and at certain points in our conversations she would not be able to tell if she was awake or dreaming. Words even now that I find hard to believe, though the temptation to give in to fantasy and the unreal so long after the fact is tempting. As Breton put it in his book *Arcanum 17*: *"In the jungle of solitude, the beautiful flick of a fan can be mistaken for paradise."* This statement couldn't be more true when applied to L. Without even trying she managed to penetrate the very core of my thoughts and desires and they intermingled and danced until they became a tangled mess that found no outlet with her. I asked myself why this happened. Though at the same time miraculous and wonderful, the vacuum of those moments spent in her presence trying hard to weave my way into her life seemed almost foolish. The strange and often frantic search for a missing person equates to a kind of personal insanity . . . Yes, the insane are always perfectly understandable only to themselves, and their actions are equally only understood by them as well. Even in this age of non-privacy, egotism, and voyeurism I can't find a trace of L. and that only leaves a void larger than before; a hole large enough for the existential devils to crawl through and laugh at me, which really they should. Yes, I should be laughing at myself if only to save myself once again from the annoyance and heaviness of depression. I've found it extremely difficult to let go of people of importance in my life. Objects, places, even books are easier to let go of than people who have touched your body, mind, or soul. L. was one of those people who even though her time within my sphere was so limited and so full of potential her absence now is almost too hard to bear, when all that really matters in life is time and the time we give over to others. Perhaps my regret has more to do with lost time than anything else, or the idea that I will in all likelihood never see her face again . . . A face, like mine, that has changed forever.

So it goes. To believe that the Universe always conspires to help you would be folly. More often than not the Universe tricks you in to believing there is a rhyme and reason to every significant event but in actuality cause and effect is nothing more than just an unsavoury taste in our mouths when things don't go our way. And yes, more often than not things don't go our way. There is no centre that grounds us in reality except perhaps the planets and stars in the sky, the rest is *chaos and disorder*. If I'm to believe in this concept then maybe, just maybe, L. will one day appear before me again, aged and wise, ready to tell me tales of strange experiences and the quotidian grind that we all share. That would be wonderful indeed, but I'm not holding my breath . . .

She initially disappeared from my life around the Feast Day of the Green Candle. I probably drank some absinthe with the Archer that day to ease the mental pain I was surely going to feel. The Archer was a notorious absinthe drinker at the time, a spoonful of sugar at the ready and a lighter to ignite the deep green. The whole of our lives at the time centred around the colour green, in fact. Cannabis sativa and the Green Goddess are a deadly combination that gives rise to bold, vivid dreams; dreams in which I would often see her off in the distance gesturing for me to follow her into the night. Getting lost in the night in Midtown could only serve to ruin me by its intoxicating flavours and eerie delights. This would be especially dangerous in the company of someone who is equally as passionate about delving into the Unknown. Even in the realm of dreams, sadness doesn't seem to vanish as one would hope. The tensions of the outer world seem to amplify in some cases, more so in the cases of missed opportunities and reckless actions, so seeing her in my dreams served no purpose other than to remind me how I tend to not follow my instincts. Instead, I give power over to the rational part of my mind which does little for me in the End. I just give birth to ghosts . . .

It wasn't until the month of Tatane, around the Feast day of Father Ubu, that I saw her again, turning my head swiftly around when I heard my name being called. There she was. Just like the first time, standing at a distance with a cigarette in her hand, leaning up against a wall, smiling shyly. I couldn't believe my luck and I could feel my heart stop briefly, sweat beginning to form on my brow. Why? Was I really that scared and anxious to speak to someone that I thought had become a spectre like so many others?

In an almost hushed tone she spoke of how, after she had left, there were times she would come to look for me, waiting on the fringes of the parkade or the doors to the stairwells hoping I would come out to smoke. Eventually giving up, effort fading into wonder at what had become of me. My heart began to melt in that moment as she described her actions, for it was the first and only time I felt that someone was just as driven to seek me out as much as I was driven to seek them out and the divide that existed between us for all those months just drifted away.

She casually wrote her number out on a scrap piece of paper and told me to call soon . . .

Weeks passed, months passed into oblivion and I did nothing. Something prevented me from touching a potential destiny, a potential whirlwind change to the weather I had to endure. Maybe it was just plain cowardice, a trait all too familiar and the subject of much debate with myself. Yes, it was fucking cowardice of the most intense kind. Yet, at some point I did make the call. Spring had fallen away or was close to falling away into the heat of summer and the Feast Days of the Cold, Solid Sun. Her voice at the other end of the telephone seemed surprised, perhaps a little annoyed I waited so long to call. Could I blame her?

Eventually the rain fell and we sat and ate noodles together, staring out the window at the people huddled under umbrellas or under newspapers, a deep silence beginning to creep over our lunch as we both felt the inevitable goodbye. She had met someone in the interim and was talking about heading for the Coast or something to that effect, which only served to make me feel incredibly stupid for not taking action, a feeling I have not been able to live down since. There have been numerous, actually countless, times I've felt stupid in my lifetime but for some reason this incident, somehow above many others, feels so much worse. Tales of loss, even minor ones such as these, are what seem to guide my life, not those grand errors which usually set people on a different path. The Void that remains is what seems to haunt me as the years pass and there is no way to fill it unless all those ghosts of people past come back to life and can assure me that all has been well . . .

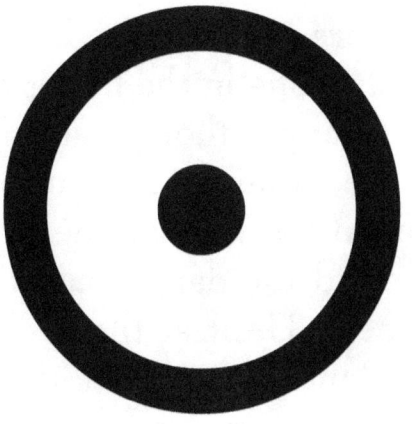

If I took apart my nightmares, what would be at the core? If I peeled back all those layers would there be a ball of light shining back at me? The barest strands of morning light reached deep into my eyes through the curtains and I would awaken to the silent house, looking at the dew on the grass, the car still missing. It's really not hard to remember those days—at least the pieces that stick so well to the grey matter—where I spent an inordinate amount of time staring at myself in the mirror. There were two mirrors in our house, one in the hallway and one in the living room, which I always found strange, though strangely inviting, for it allowed me to imitate and mold my personality. A personality always so inexplicably drawn to the obscure and the dangerous. I've called it a menacing sickness. Unfit at that point to find the Threshold, let alone contemplate the Key. I found the obscure and dangerous territory in the encyclopedias by the living room window—the danger lying in the vast knowledge that somehow felt reserved for everyone but me: nuclear energy, Aristotle, Gregor Mendel, the solar system. Yes: The Strong Force, Philosophy, Genetics, the Universe. Forbidden subjects to one so curious, sarcastic, and inevitably angry. Always a desire to write out my thoughts in magic marker on any surface like a childhood graffiti . . . unexplained

46

ailments . . . doorways . . . social neurosis . . . rainy beaches in midsummer in countries far away. These were somehow a part of my dreams and early sorrows that perhaps meant nothing, but mean more now, yet still remain transparent.

The day was before me, but it already felt empty.

"Loneliness is such a drag," as Hendrix said so poignantly on *Burning of the Midnight Lamp*. I had to get out.

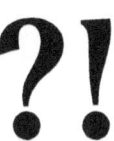

I made a silent agreement with myself as I stepped out onto the sidewalk and headed toward the centre of the Vayu: find someone to talk to, to relate to, something . . . better than reading old postcards of explicit words, so hate filled and damaging that floated around the house after the maternal figure left . . . No, those were not postcards . . . I wished they had been. My erratic habit with tobacco and VHS pornography was also doing nothing for me either, other than fogging my mind and chafing my penis. I had to get out. The cold night was a long way off but I felt it coming, silken and clean. Even as the sun shone on my young face, I could sense the night and the pistol it held in its hand, ready to shoot me the first chance it got . . .

Roussel "Instructions for 59 Drawings" . . . no. 51:

"A smartly dressed man applying the barrel of a pistol to his temple, his finger on the trigger." Or it can be stated: the Great Work is given to us divided just before the End by a statement that undertakes to explain how . . . The Marble Corridor*, which came to light after the writing of everything else, which bears a strange relationship to the work whose mechanism it reveals by covering it in an autobiographical narrative at once hasty, modest, and meticulous.

Stained glass and low light in an intimate space. A misled teen listening to circadian free jazz on a cassette player and awoken by the understated lift of anarchy coming through the cheap headphones, harnessing the dark matter of obscure art. Images of Charon the Ferryman drift across his consciousness as he steps inside the store . . .

Looking for something?

He turns and the wall of books and magazines appear like a huge hallucination, catching him off guard.

Not sure . . . Can you suggest something of interest?

The large figure laughs a hearty laugh and walks over to one of the walls where a thousand volumes stand erect, waiting to be handled with care. He steps onto a small stool and pulls one down from the top row, adjusting his glasses to check the title: *The Aleph* by Jorge Luis Borges.

This should keep you occupied for a while, I would imagine.

Holding the book in his hands he silently flips through the pages . . .

Well, do you want it or not?

Yes, yes, this will do fine thank you . . .

Feet over pavement and a rattling in the skull, eager to read the pages in relative silence. It's midday and the stomach aches. A few dollars in the pocket for a plate of waffle fries at the local diner, heavy on the seasoning salt just the way he likes it. He randomly opens the volume to a story that catches his eye . . . *The House of Asterion.*

During times of deep reflection on the past, I imagine the House on Ash Tree Lane* or the description of the House of Asterion from Borges' collection *The Aleph*, drawing the conclusion that literature, in its infinite wisdom and accuracy, views places of dwelling as unreal spaces not truly worth dwelling in at all, and its inhabitants become totally invisible in the end. I really didn't want to return home that night, or any night for that matter, but what choice did I have? I couldn't watch the dark motionless world of the Vayu forever, could I, with its intoxicating whispers and angel headed visionaries staring at the moon?

They all vomited and vanished, only to reappear the next day in a haze of suffering, leaping toward the sunlight with joy, hanging out under the eaves of the K. Hotel all battered and bleak . . .

Where was I? Beyond the fray, back at home, ready to face the end of a forgettable summer, rotting away the vestiges of my innocence in a cloud of cigarette Smoke and endless reruns. I took one long walk into the cemetery dawn of August and within three months the Vayu was behind me. She came to get me and all was put to rest as we drove out of view. All that was familiar and lovely lay tranquilized in the back of my head, only to resurface now when it is far too late to go back, for there is nothing to go back to at all.

....

Flash forward. How far? It doesn't matter. We agreed to meet in the building lobby and I loitered around feeling nervous as though the cameras were looking not just at me, but at my soul. The elevator door opened and she motioned me in; that's when I got a good look at her. She had changed, or at least she appeared to have changed. Regardless, she looked good. Her ebony skin glistened and her nice hips were accentuated by the tight yoga pants she wore. Nice smile, friendly, and a hugger. It felt good to hug someone before clawing through their Flesh. We chatted for a few minutes and she promptly let her clothes drop to the floor before sitting daintily on the edge of the bed. My mind, for all intents and purposes, felt at ease. The wind blew and howled outside the window, and icicles dangled from the eaves of the building. Her skin felt warm against my torso as she began her tongue acrobatics. Christmas was in the air, what year I don't remember, but the falling mercury stood in direct contrast to the rising of the heat within me and the chaotic pulse that seemed destined to explode at any moment. She stopped and looked up at me with a smile. Without any words or awkward action she placed herself above me and the gloom of winter seemed to disappear behind my closed eyes, her place in the cycle of pleasure Unknown to her as the grind and push gave way to climax.

In a past life I was pure, glacial spring-water.

normal women
COLD AND LONELY?

Sensual, Warm,

TESTOSTERONE

. . . the gift of a body is never one to take lightly, no matter the circumstances. She laughed and smiled as though the whole world were her oyster, which it may have been, then proceeded to spoil me again with the contours and smooth edges of her languid limbs. After I left the Vayu that summer I never imagined ever being in the comfort of another person's arms, let alone a virtual stranger. Strange times give way to strange experiences and all those years I yearned for connections of any kind the world was now giving to me in spades as though I deserved it, which to this day I really think I didn't deserve. The meaning of these encounters eluded me for a very long time, but what was apparent, at least in my own eyes, was that my shadow was rising to meet me. . . .

There is something to be learned from the night as it wraps itself around your shoulders, comfortably caressing you and allowing a quick disappearance, never considering a complete return into the arms of those you love and care about, seducing your better judgement and laughing when you take a shaking first step over a line most people care to not cross. Arcades and blinking lights of fantasy and the smell of damp basement rooms. Frescoes of Japanese bridges and samurais, lotus flowers and tiny waterfalls. The Cloak-Man eyes me like he always does as I put a quarter into *Wonderboy in Monster Land*, his nicotine stained fingers so yellow it seems as though a virus has taken hold of him.

"You only got half an hour tonight . . . I'm not staying open while you fuck around on that machine."

I only half hear his words, as I'm more concerned with getting wing-boots, armour, and bombs. The Cloak-Man groans and goes back to playing pool with the regulars who are coming down off hits of Crimson Silhouette* and Warp 9*. This is the quietest time of the night . . . Yes, night . . . narcotic . . . faces in shadow or hood . . . Darkness over the surface of the Deep/Genesis 1:2 . . . The once young kid in the urban wilderness with no provisions who endlessly wandered Salamander Road and the back alleys of the Vayu.

These were the places where I learned two things: one, how to Smoke, and two, how to buy the right Books . . .

Books have satisfied me in a way sex, drugs, music and all the rest have failed to do, but to be fair all those pleasures I've just mentioned have done much to amplify the pleasures of the text, and vice versa. As Roberto Bolaño pointed out on many occasions, he was always "happier reading than writing." I'm sure some writers would say that they enjoy the process of writing, but I believe that's a lie; all of us writers, good and bad, would much rather be flipping pages and being lost in some context other than our own, especially if it means not staring at the blank page or the blinking cursor on the computer screen.

Though it has also been said that in order to become a great writer we must read a great deal, that only by way of other people's words and ideas can we too become great. As for smoking, the Scorpion* was the first person I remember lighting a cigarette with after we found an unopened pack near the Vayu bookstore. The romance of smoke and the pull toward death were often found on the pages of Chandler, in David Lynch movies, or really anything resembling art of any kind. It seemed like a prerequisite for being taken seriously, except perhaps if you were a heavy drinker too, which of course has its own romanticism until that kills you as well. Anything worth doing will kill you in the end, I guess . . . writer, non-writer, drinker, smoker, or sex addict. Maybe it's best to be all those things wrapped up into one. In reality though, most of us writers become nothing more than a footnote, or even less than that . . .

A few years ago, after I read Enrique Vila-Matas's novel *Bartleby and Company*, I seriously contemplated giving up writing for good, which after twenty years of toil, frustration, and too much smoking would have been the *right* thing to do. But writers rarely do anything that is good for them, as a matter of fact, unless it's giving up smoking which I did ten years ago and to be perfectly honest I still miss incredibly some days. Vila-Matas' novel concerns itself with writers who give up and the nature of writing itself, two perennial themes that have plagued me over the years as a writer who has published very little and continued nonetheless perhaps just for my own amusement. I suppose the true power of the text lies in the fact that it can ruin a life as much as it can empower it, and despite feeling a sense of failure after reading that wonderful book I continued anyway . . . I mean, what the fuck else was I going to do?

The burden of writing lies not just in the act itself but also in the tradition one inherits the minute they pick up a pen. Once the writer actually starts to write in earnest, the glaring eyes of the giants of Literature look upon them as perhaps the next victim. Like any tradition, to be a recognized person of merit is a large task indeed. Nabokov—he too, being one of the greats—gave the following criteria for becoming a major writer: "There are three points of view from which a writer can be considered: he may be considered as a storyteller, as a teacher, and as an enchanter. A major writer combines these three—storyteller, teacher, enchanter—but it is the enchanter in him that predominates and makes him a major writer." Well said. I know from reading so many of his novels that what he is saying is true, and that developing those three qualities, or in particular the first two, is where the hard work of editing and rewriting come in. As for enchantment, that is the product of *destiny* and probably out of the hands of any writer worth his salt. Destiny bestows enchantment amongst the greats of any art, and to some a little more is given, like in the cases of Shakespeare, Dante, or Cervantes. Writing of that level and calibre goes beyond mere enchantment and enters a realm even higher: the mythical. Yes, this is what the potential writer is burdened with from the moment they are pushed out of the literary womb: a horrendous chance to fail. Out of the hundreds of books that I've read there are very few authors that I can say are bad storytellers. I say this because even the smallest child can be a great storyteller, so the ability to tell a story well is really a quality that belongs to a large part of humanity, and yes, some can tell better stories but I've met very few that are what one would call bad, and even fewer *write* bad stories. I think my dislike of a particular writer has more to do with the content or form of the story rather than their ability to write it, but in saying that I also think of what Jack Kerouac said: "It ain't whatcha write, it's the way atcha write it." That quote alone brings me to the conclusion that my opinions on literature are varied and idiotic, if not downright ridiculous.

So really, in the end, content does not matter if one can write in such a way to make it interesting, and if that's the case then the true masters of literature would be the ones who took the most benign, boring subjects and created masterpieces out of them, am I right? Perhaps, but we all know that interpreting subjects of such magnitude, particularly the whole of literature, is a tricky endeavour and there is no right answer when it comes to these large subjects, but we can certainly try.

That brings us to teaching as the second quality, where the writer uses the depth of their experiences and observations to give us a better understanding of the world around us and, hopefully, ourselves. My main annoyance with legendary literary texts is the quality surrounding them regarding "universal themes" and the idea that the definition of what makes these works of art great in the first place is their universal appeal and longevity. There is a grain of truth in this, as there is to most arguments, but what this is also supposing is that these works should appeal to *everyone* on some level *due to their universality*. More often than not, these books annoyed me and I found them — or at least the idea of them — boring. With the exception of the three mythical writers I mentioned earlier — Shakespeare, Dante, and Cervantes — the so-called classics seemed so far removed from my experience that I couldn't understand what their appeal continued to be.

I think my opinions on the classics began to change once I purchased, quite on a whim, the complete essays of Montaigne at one of the many used Midtown bookstores. A massive book, I flipped through the table of contents and searched for a subject that both caught my eye and was relatively short. At this point I wasn't sure if I would even keep the book, but my eyes fell upon

On Idleness. Yes, the essay was indeed short and to the point, but something in Montaigne's writing spurred me on, leading me into the core of his writing that seemed not only insightful and reflective, but melancholic as well. I saw the man forming around these essays, which I understood he rewrote over a number of years, adding and reforming them into perfect slices of the human condition.

What I realized as I read more of his essays —which I still need to complete—is that as a young reader so offended by the 'boring' subject matter of the classics, I didn't realize that much of what I deemed to be useless was writing of *experience and maturity*, two qualities that only now I have begun to develop. Despite this late blooming of appreciation I could never say for certain that any degree of universality flooded my soul and mind from reading those essays, but yes, Montaigne was indeed *teaching* me something about *myself*, not necessarily about universal themes that bind us all. Death binds us; taxes bind us; but *interpretations* of universal themes don't, they simply broaden our perceptions of certain universal phenomena and in the off chance within our readings we may see someone else's experiences as a reflection of our own. Was Montaigne a major writer? Yes, of course. He developed and made popular a literary form that is used everyday. Was he a teacher? Yes. Did he enchant? That remains to be seen. Have I managed to come to any real conclusion regarding the qualities of major writers???

The third quality is a tricky one for me because the more I read the more I think I disagree with Nabokov on what makes a major writer. Dostoyevsky is considered a major writer. He was also a very dry storyteller . . . Did he teach? Yes. He tackled the psychology of faith, of violence, of mere being. Did he enchant? In my opinion, no. I cannot recall a sentence in *Notes from Underground, The Devils, The Gambler,* or *Crime and Punishment* as ever having enchanted me. Do I think those books are amazing psychological studies? Yes, indeed I do, but I would never call Dostoyevsky an enchanter. Few would, I think. So who enchants? Is the basis for major writing really just a matter of being a master of one of those three qualities that Nabokov mentioned? Perhaps. I consider an enchanter a writer who touches your soul with their words, one that makes you *feel* in an entirely different way than you're used to while at the same time changing your perception of yourself or your reality.

In a rather morbid twist, one of the first writers I encountered who did this to me was Kafka, but when I discovered Japanese literature in my early twenties it was Ryūnosuke Akutagawa whose fluid short stories truly altered my view on the concept of suicide. Considered the Father of the Short Story in Japan, he committed suicide at the age of 35 in 1927. His suicide note, titled *Note to a Certain Old Friend* is one of the most enchanting pieces I've ever read. At merely a page, he managed to convince me in the most eloquent and mysterious way that the final act he was committing was indeed for the best. I've read it many times; sometimes in sorrow, and sometimes in the best of moods and it retains its power over me not only because these were the final words of a literary master, but also because it was *honest*. So maybe that is what makes a major writer: a sense of honesty and a lack of pretension, and a world laid naked at one's feet when their words are read . . .

I suppose this brings us to the final category to where only the truly rare dwell, the mythical. As previously stated, destiny bestows much on certain writers and in the case of Dante, Shakespeare, and Cervantes, who stand in my personal view as mythical writers, a little more is given. What is that 'little more?' Mystery. The Unknown, the Invisible. If we are to value Nabokov's three aspects of a major writer for the sake of this final argument, those three men are the epitome — along

with several others I'm sure — that have the qualities of storytelling, teaching, and enchantment. So
yes, I'm of the opinion that along with the curva-
ture of their destinies and their remarkable skills
that the mystery surrounding them is what puts
them in that final realm of the mythical.

They are my holy trinity of Literature . . .
untouchable, elusive, and hidden in the crevices of
history where only *their work* stands as what is
important. Destiny never called upon me to take
the reins of the Word, but I gather them together
nonetheless, perhaps in vain. So it goes . . .

RYAN MADEJ

THIS IS A VISUAL TRIBUTE TO THE HOSTS, SETS, STUNTS, AND CONTESTANTS THAT STILL OCCUPY A PLACE IN OUR NATIONAL PSYCHE

BLIND

UNDER SENTENCE OF DEATH

sitting behind the cupboard door, listening, not too sure of what he should do, obviously he's waiting for him to come *of a dirty seventy-two-old tramp and the blonde twenty-year-old foxhunter Third Class. The camera pans to the couple on the bed. Lennox peers dimly round the cupboard door, on the inside of which is pasted a photograph from a magazine of two astronauts in space. He watches* Dennis Anson he

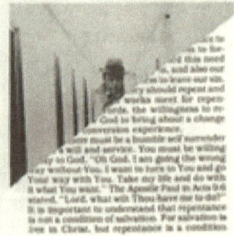

face to ... ... his to lis- ... ...d that need ... ...is, and also our ... ...se to leave out sin. ... ...y should repent and ... ... works meet for repen- ... ...tanls. the willingness to re- ... ... God to bring about a change ... ... conversion experience. ... ...here must be a humble self surrender ... ...s will and service. You must be willing ... ...p to God. "Oh God. I am going the wrong ... ...ray without You. I want to turn to You and go ... ...Your way with You. Take my life and do with ... ...it what You want." The Apostle Paul in Acts 9:6 ... stated, "Lord, what wilt Thou have me to do?" It is important to understand that repentance is not a condition of salvation. For salvation is ...ree in Christ, but repentance is a conditio...

END GAMES

66

So it began in earnest: living with the maternal figure. Gone were her idealistic thoughts about me attending an academic school where everything was shipshape and sharp; gone were the thoughts of me becoming something. She never said it, but I could see it in her eyes; gone were the feelings of family, and gone were the tears that had so flooded our former home where the schism began. Gone. I just kept saying it over and over in my head until it made sense but I don't think it ever did.

There was some redemption on the horizon though. As I stepped through the doors of the school I would be reunited with the Lion*. That is the essence of the Tao: in the midst of extreme Yin or Yang, there still remains a portion of the opposite force which lingers within . . . the Lion was that portion, a most needed remedy for survival. He was one of my oldest friends, the counterpart to the Scorpion. So it was: the Lion and the Fishes adrift on a cruel sea for the next three years. The lonesome, cool eyes of girls in sweaters occupied my thoughts, along with the displeasure of mathematics. Kids high on LSD and benzedrine, pot and PCP, walked the halls sunk in visions, drained and tattered, wailing on rooftops of cars while I ate Sunburst noodles from a styrofoam container and chewed Bubble King. Those days seemed long and lonely at first, even as me and the Lion made endless treks around the school, our conversations forgotten. My life outside the metal fence felt so alien and strange, now that I was across town in a new world. All communications were cut from what I knew best. All I had were a box of cassette tapes and a little stereo I had gotten for Christmas a few years before. I don't even remember having a bed for the longest time, only a sleeping bag in which to curl up in at night. Inward the energy went, deeper and deeper ...

I craved her ~~ass~~ mind. She was hungry and brilliant and I wish I could have been ~~blown~~ killed by her. By all accounts she was the first girl I had massive erotic overtones for. I used to buy her Bubble King which is part of the reason I bought it in the first place. Filipino girl, honour student at that . . . seemingly popular, with a pretty smile. A supernatural ecstatic joyride erupted in me. A wet dream? Regardless, I wanted her memories and her lips. In all honesty I could give her nothing in return other than my simple generosities. Maybe that was enough. My penis would have to wait along with all the others who craved just as much as I did, the sick fucks that we were. Always a need to jack off in the midst of spring with the cool evening breeze floating in through the window and the sounds of the midnight trains moving through the darkness. I wrote obscene odes to her name at the silent library that sat on the Square.

Ode 1: Venus in Chains

. . . ~~vagina shaven~~ like a dynamo . . . floating across the lonesome sea and through the impulses of shining windows, the moon glowing. Dusty rooms where we meet or pass through, into back-yards, subways, or boxcars, doing peyote together at dawn while undressing ourselves ~~for the inevitable fuck~~ . . . shadows vibrating and our brains screaming and smoking through the cracks of dreams and snow. We are caught in the small town rain inhaling narcotic tobacco, ash falling off the roof ~~and onto our flaming genitals~~, ranting and crying in delight celebrating our telepathy, our nightmares, our madness for one another . . . a deep tragedy ~~as we talk and fuck continuously on drugs~~ . . . finally escaping our generation and our intellects for a life in the Caribbean, the machinery of our brains dead from pleasure. Gone . . . just like the all the rest of it, but it feels good to finally get it off my chest.

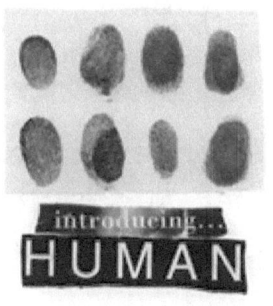

Tripping on hormones was almost worse than tripping on Mary Jane. The dull throb just seconds away. My understanding of the world was limited by my own teen self-absorption. The maze of feelings and dread that seemed to follow me melted around me for the next three years. Summer in the early '90s: a compulsion to spread ideas, but my jigsawed mind needed some manipulating. I felt unwell. Two events would serve to change this situation in a personally dramatic fashion: meeting the Irishman* and The Archer*. Both of them appeared suddenly, like apparitions on a cold evening. One brought drugs, the other insight. Not a bad combination considering the circumstances. Good people on a Bad Planet. Disconnecting the wires that had been plunged into my head . . .

The Irishman came into my life through the backdoor, like a thief, and he told me so. He did break and enters, petty theft, and probably a great deal more that I could only imagine. I befriended him in a class full of nobodies and people aching to fit in to certain mold. I suppose I wanted to do the same, but not with any of those fucking jokers. He knew I wouldn't narc on him, mainly because I had no desire to, plus judging a person by their actions seemed like a foolish pursuit at such a young age. I mean, from my own perspective I expected the same in return, and that is what I received in full from the situation. That, and perhaps more than I bargained for, but more nonetheless.

So began lines of disconnected thoughts and wishes, shallow plots and images not meant for mainstream consumption. It felt as though a hundred doves had been let loose in my skull ☼ . . . no longer muzzled by a strange system of control . . . I guess I began to check out . . . I smoked hashish with him* and the world began to shift . . . the heavy lead of my former life began to slowly transmute into gold. The Great Work is one's Life as each day spreads and spirals out like a Fibonacci Sequence on fire.

My modus operandi was to be a dust dragon, or an astral strangler. A 15-year-old Faust ready for action. Fuck mathematics, fuck language arts, fuck science. I was into *The Prisoner*, Kurt Vonnegut, and T.S. Eliot. Yes, what might have been always lies dormant behind the wall of sleep which is our lives, reminding us that the door we didn't choose still lies unopened and the one we did open is where we are now, regretting nothing but cursing so much that followed. The world was finally mine and I began to wonder where the Key lay, but I was too stoned most of the time to figure that out in any real way, shape, or form . . . Δ and Ω.

Somewhere in that span of three years I took up the pen in earnest. There was a summer in there, what year I cannot remember, that was the catalyst for a lengthy withdrawal of sorts from the mundane 'real world.' To write meant to live; to live meant to write. A simple means of survival, at least in a mental sense, where the direct action of the pen took the place of impulse, fantasy, and good taste. The blank page became the canvas for all I withheld from the world, just as it does now, only then it seemed so much more *necessary*. In the present, it means that I still find it necessary.

Enter the Archer: a self-deprecating but natural style in word and action. A sea of good ideas that floated on an ocean of paranoia. He needs to avoid the morgue at this point; too traumatized, too many blows to the head, too much abuse, too much pot, too much whiskey. The more I think about him, the more it saddens me. I get acid reflux and the tears are always on the verge of erupting from my eyes. He slipped through the cracks and became a light and guidance in the middle of a gargantuan absence. At first it seemed like he was just hanging around like an unwanted visitor (which he was, in my eyes at least), but as time went on I knew he was there to stay. A fixture on the couch, a spectre in the kitchen, a wild philosopher on quiet evenings during the summer. A friend, a kind of father, a comfort to a boy in need. Talk of Pyramids and Sport, WW2 and the brilliance of Pink Floyd or Led Zeppelin. The list went on and so did our discussions about everything above and below us, and as the months turned into years I reflected on how he gave me so much without any sort of expectations, salutations, or anything for that matter. Yet, I respected him a great deal, even as the maternal figure set to make the home situation one of confusion and bitter feelings. At some points I imagine them as being happy, but inherently unhappy people only seek out unhappy people. People to prop them up or to be sounding boards for their delusions and neurotic behaviour.

Such was the case. A cycle of repetitious nonsense that has only led to decay. Though amongst the chaos there is also a degree of order—a semblance of sanity where there is none. My room became a happy cell where I took refuge. My supplies were simple: books, television, pipe tobacco, and music to soothe me. What is so regretful about the nature of memory is the fact that what we want to remember most is what becomes the most obscured, whereas the most biting and despicable of our memories are the ones that flash before our mind's eye, but that one true summer I had by myself in the sweltering heat with the windows always open still retains a gloss of vividness. I can picture my red metal bar desk with my pile of manuscript pages flapping in the breeze and smell the aroma of a fresh packet of Captain Black whose smell stuck to my fingers for days from rolling cigarettes while watching French cinema in the evenings. My almost spartan existence was punctuated by a deep longing for the Unknown, the periphery of which I had only begun to stand on. It was there in my room where the Library came to life, for what better way to lose oneself to the void than to read. Somewhere below me in that townhouse, where the cries and voices of our obnoxious neighbours filtered through the walls so easily, the maternal figure sat, unconcerned. I always loved her for that while at the same time despising it in my heart of hearts. So it goes. Resentment is not the goal in the End.

Somewhere in this miasma of exploration—meaning writing deep into the nights—a gift fell into my lap from the father figure, who by this point in the narrative had become something of a ghost. His voice would occasionally be on the other line of the telephone, sounding remote and alien, reminding me of a brief meet-up or family dinner of some kind. So many times I sat on a Sunday afternoon in the food court near the Square eating noodles while I waited for him to arrive. The strange dichotomy of having the Archer on one side and a ghost on the other seemed almost appropriate the more I pondered the situation. Is it not the balance of things to have fullness in one aspect of your life while having close to nothing on the other? Or maybe this was just the pattern of my life whose trajectory has not changed in this respect. Anyway, the father figure once bestowed upon me a real gift; a gift so proper that as I look back on it, the significance and the joy that it gave me almost made up for his absence.

The gift was an electric typewriter. He had found it second hand in his wanderings and leap at the chance to give it to me—the weight of the machine itself was staggering for someone like myself, who at 150 pounds found lugging it across the city something of a challenge. The machine was loud, and many a night I could be heard snapping the keys as I wrote *The Trench*, that sickening disease of a work that consumed so much of my life for so long that much of it is a blur. What it gave me though was a sense of purpose, a direction forward, and on those warm summer nights as I sipped vermouth and tapped at the keys, the sound of distant trains haunting my thoughts, I often thought of the father figure and how in many ways I felt betrayed but at the same time elevated by this man who gave me life. So that became the paradigm for a long while: the Archer on the left and the father figure on the right, playing an invisible chess match that neither of them knew they were playing. I would stand by the window and blow Smoke into the evening air, finally settling into a new phase where only the Word made sense . . .

The Black Light District

I managed to stifle a laugh as I stared at my image in the mirror. The winter did little to settle my soul; as a matter of fact, I felt more unsettled in the winter months when the vacuum of cold arrived, giving way to introspective landscapes. Grim atmosphere, wind and shake, waiting for a train that may never come. I had been invited one early morning in January by Miss Feather to dine between her legs under the auspices of good fortune told to me from the pages of the *I Ching*. She lived in the silent, remote section of the city known as the Black Light District because of its proximity to the Grand Cemetery and its reputation for murders of a sexual nature. The dim luminescence from snowcapped street lamps lapped at my face, their penumbra fading even as I looked at them made me shiver a little more. To the West, the shell of a former life, silent and grey, immovable and graceless.

I breathed deeply, feeling my lungs ache as a result of the cold that trickled over the Threshold. A crow cawed in the distance as if to mock me. I would have been better off walking, but I've always feared the trails of the valley that wind around the Velox*. The empty dawn light fell over me and I was reminded of my own greasy charm and average penis, wandering the streets high on codeine and gin, tapping the inbox of my mind and believing I was in Paris and not the Ends of the Earth. The scene never really gets old does it? Deep meaningful dreams with my eyes wide open, bewitched by the smell of ordinary whiskey and Smoke.

She answered the door with a smile—a half-hearted smile—and proceeded to light a candle while calmly undressing down to her panties, fondling her left breast, while I had barely taken off my coat. It all seemed so false and the potential sting of an early morning discourse before sex seemed like strange foreplay, but being under the influence of my own twisted experiments, I fell for the trap.

The difficulty came in paying attention to the words we spoke to one another. Not only that, she was half-naked before me, which reminded me of the famous picture of Duchamp playing chess with a young Eve Babitz I saw once in reproduction.

-So what have you been up to lately? I mean, it's been a long time since we last saw one another.

I had to think about that because so much seemed to be swirling around in my head.

-Plenty. Though, to be perfectly honest, all I can think about is the perfect roundness of your breasts, which I feel slightly guilty about, really.

A nasal laugh echoed through the room.

-Why would you feel guilty about that? That is why you're here, right?

I thought it might be, but at the same time I just wanted to keep warm, preferably in the arms of a semi-stranger. Then I wondered if I had said all that out loud. I needed something more than Flesh, but what? She was the closest thing I had to a friend at that time, but a friend who knew so little about me, about the City, about anything . . .

-Do you want a beer or something?

-The sun has barely risen and you're asking if I want a beer?

-Well, do you?

-No, I want to fuck . . . is that too much to ask at this point?

She shot me an icy glare from across the room, but really we both knew that was all we were going to do at this point or any point in the future, though the future seemed less and less like a possibility for me once the Nexus had opened. She became a point on an imaginary grid that stretched from the tips of my fingers to the edge of my vision, where all kinds of tiny details seemed to dovetail together in a cosmic stew served just for me. Something else was distracting me though. Oh yes, the naked woman sitting across from me.

She appeared beside me, smelling like a mixture of jasmine and mint, a refreshing bouquet considering her apartment seemed to carry a death vapour. Some of the locals used to tell me that Bastion Perrot and his acolytes built the city outwards from the Great Cemetery in order to harness the power of the dead in their rituals, but these same people would laugh after saying this, leaving me in a state of wonder as to what his intentions really were, which no one really knows. At the same time I began to wonder if the naked maiden beside me was a demon of some sort. Her eyes were bloodshot, but that probably had more to do with the alcohol she had been consuming beforehand and not a single bit of evil, but who knew? She slurred:

-Well, are we going to do this or not?

Her face felt warm against my cheek and the smell of mint and jasmine were suddenly replaced by the odours of stale beer and nicotine. I stuck my tongue in her mouth anyway as it seemed like I was wasting my time if I didn't and wasting time is the worst thing a person can do in life, perhaps next to murdering someone. For a split second before I succumbed to the void of her vaginal fluids I thought that maybe she was the one who had taken so many lives around the District . . .

"Let it happen," I said to myself as she climbed above me. The swift slice of a knife hidden under a pillow, a poisoned needle, anything to draw me closer to the dead who seemed to haunt my dreams and clog my thoughts during the day. Then, nothing. A quick throb into the vastness of her womb and Nothing. A peaceful cigarette and empty talk about the heavy winter that had descended on Midtown in the last month. I lay there in the near darkness of the morning wishing I was somewhere else, not because of my decision to fuck her but for reasons I could not explain.

-You want to go again, or are you too spent?

-What?

-I said do you want to go again or are you too spent?

-Too spent. I should go . . . places to be.

-Where do you need to be this early in the morning anyway?

-Definitely not here.

To Spike Spiegel (In Memoriam)

I was younger then, I wasn't afraid of anything, I didn't think about dying for a second. I thought I was invincible. Then I met some girl. I wanted to live, I started to think like that; for the first time I was afraid of death. I had never felt like that before.

-Spike Spiegel

The imaginary worlds we fall prey to often give birth to characters who touch our souls in a particular way, who might even fulfill the criteria set out at the beginning. Do I dare make the assumption that perhaps a perfect character—at least in my mind—would embody the four elements I described in the beginning? No, I wouldn't dare make that assumption, for who I am to make any assumptions about anything? Well, Spike Spiegel, bounty hunter and philosopher, has come close over the years. Of course, anyone who is familiar with the legendary anime *Cowboy Bebop* knows that Spike is not only the epitome of what makes a character cool, but on another level a tragic figure in the whole scheme of the series itself.

Here was a man I felt a kinship with, perhaps because of the somewhat hard-boiled overtones and jazzy textures that the series exudes in spades, but also because he was a character who faced the

Unknown with wit, charm, and a fierceness that by the end of the 24 episode run had managed to fill me with a sense of sadness when he inevitably met his end. Like Joseph K in *The Trial*, or John Shade in *Pale Fire*, Spike Spiegel etched himself on my soul. Perhaps that is the fundamental function of Art: to create something so vivid and alive from the imaginary that it transcends the imaginary. Maybe this is obvious. The series itself is widely considered a masterpiece and is often found near or at the top of many all-time anime lists. It would be easy to say that Spike was somewhat of a romantic in every sense of the word—considering what he said in the above quote—but that would be too easy of an interpretation for our liking, wouldn't it, my friends?

The love he had for Julia, the subject of the quote above, and the hatred he had for his former friend, the gangster Vicious, shows a classic dichotomy so deeply entrenched in the human condition that one may ask themselves if love and hate are really the only two forces that have any bearing on our often quotidian existence. Spike, however—in his sometimes snide, sometimes philosophical remarks—felt as though he was dreaming and that his mission was to find out if this were true or not, thus sending him into the Unknown without any fear of consequence.

Perhaps that in itself is a truly romantic notion, albeit a somewhat foolish one. Then again, humans commit many foolish actions in order to find truth, or at least some interpretation of truth. I like to think that his pursuit was not really made out of love per se, but it became the motivating force to send to him into action, a situation that we find ourselves in all the time. Humans need a motivation to exceed notions of themselves or they fall into decadence, spreading their energy thin until they no longer exist at all.

To say that I was saddened by the end of the series would be an understatement. I felt a deep pain as though I had lost a close friend, a feeling I've had so many times reading books . . . But to see this *ending* visually mapped out was almost too much to bear. Of course this sounds melodramatic, but one has to understand that a commitment to art, with all its artifice and falsity, still carries human emotion as the only guide. The death of an imaginary character can be of equal tragedy, I'm sure. I include my reflections on Spike as an extension of the Library, that great source of all things that gives us dimension and clarity in the midst of this strangeness. Rest easy, Spike.

Klexos*—the Art of Dwelling on the Past

As you enter the city, a man carrying a jar of water will meet you. Follow him to the house that he enters.

-Luke 22:10

A warm current of light upon the empty path that leads into the heart of Midtown strikes me every morning as the burgeoning day settles into my mind and heart. How I got here is irrelevant, but after a few hits of hash the newly born day quickly becomes a fishbowl. This is the Smoke, as revealed to me by the Irishman, not as a dampening agent for depressive thoughts, but rather as a Key to something else altogether. Consciousness expansion is not limited to an acceptance of 'well wishing' toward others or a 'connection to the Universe,' but rather, in some instances, a destruction of our perceptions of the Universe; a tool for dismantling rather than building.

Aleister Crowley, despite his many failings and somewhat apocryphal exploits, dared to place consciousness expansion at the heart of magickal practice, wherein the operator leaves their conception of the Universe open and doesn't make assumptions about its creation or our place within its confines. Instead, our consciousness—the Key, so to speak—is the playground for serious investigation into what we call reality. Crowley's own notorious use of drugs from hashish and mescaline to heroin seemed to serve this purpose in his magickal rituals—sexual or otherwise—even though it probably served to feed his madness as well. Though no one would go so far as to say he was a good human being, his writings and belief in the *potential* of humankind carried that familiar Nietzschean flavour with him no matter what he chose to do. Somehow this all bled into the following years . . .

Nothing seemed plausible for some time in those years following the grimness of the separation until I reunited with my old compatriots in the fall of 1995 . . . the Lion, the Scorpion, the Hunter, and the Ikthus, my long lost brother of different blood. From the point of view of optimism, reuniting with them on an intellectual level and, one could say, playful level, gave me a newfound strength to write seriously for the first time. It seems now—nearly two decades on—to come full circle and I see the past for what it was: an eerie phenomenon, equal parts darkness and light.

Friendship can do away with most pain, in much the same way sex or drugs can, meaning that if the friendship is of good quality, the pain is sure to recede. The Lion and the Scorpion shared a great deal of mental, physical, and to a certain degree, spiritual space with me from the time we first knew one another at the tender age of five or six, and as our friendship rekindled itself—even though we still saw one another a fair amount outside the classroom—the weight of the previous three years slowly began to slide off of me and the air of adventure began to surface once more. The Scorpion always made me feel good, which is a really simplistic way of saying I've always had a deep affection for him, but the humour and the desire he has always had to push the limits began to do wonders.

The Scorpion is the sly one, just as a real scorpion might be before they strike, and from this always came a wellspring of exuberance where we discussed plots of movies, the occasional book, or the bloody history of comic book characters who stay permanently etched in his mind. Despite the closeness we have shared all these years with the many swirls and dives into depravity that may be left for another book, I've always felt that I don't really know him all that well and that the very edges of what truly makes him who he is will forever remain obscured to me. But I suppose it's like this with everyone, right? There is always that elusive side of our closest compatriots we always wonder about, despite our greatest efforts to pry into them with the utmost gentleness. Still, I continue to wonder . . .

Which brings me to the familiar feeling of nostalgia, which science tells us is so important because it makes us feel good. Within my circle the seeds of nostalgia have grown from the tiniest saplings into almost monstrous trees in recent years, perhaps for no other reason than with age and responsibility we find a slow pushing away begin to take hold as we age, ripen, and eventually wither. Of course, in the grand scheme we are still relatively young, but at the same time there are not as many opportunities to create new memories so we tend to dwell on old ones. I guess it would be no surprise then that a lot of our activities over the years have centred around the Smoke and consciousness expansion. The Scorpion has always seemed to lead the way in some way, shape, or form, letting us in on the delights that come with the dropping of LSD or the vagaries of doing cocaine. He is the closest person I know who could resemble Hunter S. Thompson in any meaningful way, and that in itself is an accomplishment. He is in possession of a special excitement and passion for living that I envy and for all intents and purposes I associate him the most with the Smoke.

The same cannot be said about the Lion, who in even his proudest moments still is able to conceal himself and lay in the grass unnoticed. Like the Sun, which the Lion represents, he believes the world revolves around him, though not in a pretentious fashion. He is too rough around the edges to be concerned with lofty ideas and ways of doing things, but he finds his centre among the rest of us, his twirling satellites. Sometimes brash but often funny, I look to him and see my youth spread out before me. My memories of him are always vibrant and cheery and often I'm reminded of the countless walks we took together to and from school, late nights in the pool hall, and eating donair meat across Midtown's dark landscape. But like the Scorpion there is a connection to the Smoke as well, for one of my most memorable highs was spent with him as we sat in my room on a spring day two decades ago grooving to Zeppelin and laughing our faces off. That was a bonding moment like no other.

The problem with memory — at least in my case — is the fact that I always question the validity of the particular memory I'm dwelling on, simply because I can't be sure the progress of time and space has served to change the details to the way I want to remember them, which is pure and unchanged. Even the memories I have just brought forth are lacking in detail within my mind, leaving only the ragged skeletons of a once perfect moment. On the other hand, the moments are still perfect, for at least I have retained a semblance of what has brought me joy, despite the transparent quality they have taken on. Can I blame the Smoke for that? No. I can only blame myself for not remembering like Proust would have, given the opportunity.

Crowley said "every act is a magickal act" and it would appear that through the use of certain Key substances that act itself takes on a slightly deeper meaning. Reality gives way to dream and the words spoken between friends become not only memories but a *mantra* that must be repeated. So here I repeat . . .

I spent a span of seven years living with the Hunter in the Northern quarter of Midtown—a far cry from the inner workings of The Square or The Waterfront Jazz Market. The Northern Quarter was the quiet handiwork of Hanz Overbeck, the best friend and acolyte of Bastion Perrot, a district dedicated to the Earth, if I remember correctly. In any event, the area is noteworthy for its bridges that link the deep valley system with the rest of the city, as well as numerous esoteric libraries Overbeck built as areas for study. Most have fallen into disuse owing to a lack of interest, however the city government still puts money toward upkeep and general maintenance. The Hunter and I often used to take walks through the valley, the smell of the Smoke with us quite constantly. For the better part of a year, when millennium fever seemed to have subsided, we spent the majority of our money on freeing ourselves from the mundane through the Smoke, very often philosophizing and analyzing our lives like so many do under its influence.

It was all very carefree and for a period I felt something akin to happiness. The fog we created around ourselves was enough to stave off bad feelings and probably did more to unburden me from the bonds of anti-depressants I had taken for a time. We accomplished so little in that time frame, though at the same time it became quite clear to me that it would have to End in an apocalyptic fashion. Though, when it did come to an End it was something closer to T.S. Eliot's words from *The Hollow Men*: ". . . This is the way the world ends/ Not with a bang but with a whimper." After seven years, I moved out and into uncertain waters . . .

Though the details of the period that followed remain obscured, whether through my own reluctance or as a result of the progress and ravages of time, I somehow managed to find my way back to myself with less damage than expected. Perhaps it was then the true deconstruction started, when I began to reconstruct myself. The greatest asset during those years in the metaphorical wilderness was, by far, the Ikthus himself, the other Fish, the rational being who has far more love within him than myself. We too shared the Smoke, but for us it felt like more than just a bonding or a deconstruction, it held some other meaning that eluded our grasp. One of my fondest memories is of a late summer evening during an electrical storm. We had parked his car on the far edge of one of Midtown's larger parks. The air was still but the sky was lit with energy and light, the cloud of Smoke surrounded our faces and I felt like a spectre looking at another spectre as though we were the only two non-corporeal beings left on Earth. I cannot recall what we discussed that evening, yet I can recall the low hum of *Black Milk* coming from the speakers as the comfortable silence eventually set it . . . it was perfect and perhaps that was the true magickal act: the one that does not involve contrived rituals but the symbolic nature of friendship powering it from the start.

*

Flesh 5: Princess R.

Of course there are differences between the Flesh of one woman and another, but the true differences don't lie in the size and shape of a breast, or the taste of the Triangle, but perhaps in the subtle movements and sureness in these movements. Princess R. was the kind of woman who carried her physical gifts with an eerie grace. She told me on a number of occasions that her career in exotic dancing is what gave rise to her fearless languidness. I had never seen her perform for she forbade a person—reasonable or not—to watch her dance naked. I found this at odds with the fact she offered herself so easily to me, the reader of books, or as she called me: the Worm.

She felt drawn to me, as least as far as I could surmise, for my ease of conversation and not my cock, though surprisingly she still played with it from time to time if only to keep the conversation going. I remember her telling me that wintering in Midtown was always a difficult experience, not only because of the sudden changes in the weather, but the also the fact that so many sickening stories regarding the City seemed to reach out beyond the walls and into the ears of strangers and foreigners alike. Perhaps she believed I had knowledge of these 'stories,' though in reality I knew nothing more than she did, mainly because I didn't dare believe the legends and myths regarding hauntings and the like . . . No, something deeper lay at the heart of the city, but I quickly dismissed those thoughts when she placed my hands on her naked buttocks which quickly warmed my frigid digits that had been chapped by the late January winds. She whispered in my ear:

-Who is this Bastion Perrot I hear so much about?

-The short answer is he was Midtown's founder along with three others who came over with him from Europe back in the 1800's. Trust me, you don't want the long answer . . .

Turning onto her back, she stared at the ceiling in silence for a few moments before turning back over to me and placing her hand on my limp penis.

-No, I want the long answer . . . Tell me.

The warmth of her hand and the hardness of her painted nails was enough for me to speak in slow, modest tones, trying desperately to recall what I had learned so many years ago in a handful of books that were eventually traded in for better ones. Really, I played dumb as much as possible as I didn't really want to speak, leaving out all the apocrypha.

-Well, he was one of those mysterious types, as far as can be surmised by what was written by himself and others, wanting nothing more than to discover the secrets of the old alchemists. He came here with his wife, his best friend, and an acquaintance of his wife's, and settled in to build this city in their own collective vision.

She looked puzzled and the movement of her hand slowed almost to a standstill, her eyes narrowing as the words eventually came to her bright red lips.

-It's hard to believe someone would go to all that trouble and, on top of that, drag people along with him in order to do it in the first place. Or perhaps what is more absurd is the fact that others followed him at all. I mean, who does that, right?

"Exactly," I said to myself. Who does that? Who has that kind of power and influence over people, who can make them alter the course of their own existence in order to follow them? I wanted to be that kind of person, the one with the proud shoulders and charming smile, but sadly it was not meant to be, mostly on account of of my own neurosis.

She looked at me and began to stroke harder and faster in silence, perhaps because I just naturally let the conversation die as a result of my own inner digressions. Perhaps the oddest thing I discovered about my time with Princess R. and the Others is that I could talk with them in such an easy and forthright way without the usual burden that came from baring myself to supposedly closer individuals. There were no expectations with her and that made it so easy to breathe in a the most comfortable way.

Still, it solved nothing in the End. She melted away like the rest. A victim of her own beauty.

The Johari Window

Hidden

The muted, almost hushed quality that an illness brings with it has two consequences: one being the hopeless turn inward familiar to many creative people, but also a glimpse of the world through the shutters, so often missed by the hustle and bustle brought into our lives. During those times Midtown seemed far more vulnerable and less mysterious which made me swear off illness for good. The deep inherent need for mystery and intrigue lay at the root of my problems. Finding the answers in others or in situations not worth mentioning—other than the fact they involved a lot of nakedness—has been the driving force behind a dissociation that I've created within myself in the last handful of years.

A need to strangle and pull; to force and be forced; to incite a kind of mental violence upon myself and others, whether they be friend or foe. Not maliciously, but as a way of *understanding*. There is something to behold not only in the sight of one's own blood, but also in the blood of others . . .

A desire to bleed oneself out of *pleasure* and not despair is ~~fucking satisfying~~ not safe, let alone recommended; a desire to bleed others is ~~clearly~~

~~insane, or at the very least a little disturbing~~ what one thinks about in times of utter anguish or in the midst of a good laughing fit when one's emotions are at their most tangible.

Who did I bleed other than myself? Who did I want to bleed?

It all goes back to a time that has fallen prey, like so many other memories, to the vague and obscure, where the tiny fragments gather together like rodents in a nest.

Beyond the common lies the rare, the fringe, the Threshold. One night I caught a glimpse of it from a distance. Mantra Hand made an appearance that night—the first one I can actually recall—and his appearance was just as I had imagined it from all I had heard about him. He had a companion—a pretty one at that, which is no surprise. I had been invited to a fetish show in the centre of Midtown not far from Salamander Road, clearly over-looking the High Gate Bridge. The atmosphere seemed suited to this man who knew everyone there but few could really describe. He wore black dress pants and a tight white t-shirt with sus-penders, glistening Italian leather shoes, and held a walking cane with a dragon hilt. Mostly he sat in silence with his model-like companion and sipped what appeared to be scotch and water, a sense of deep impatience on his brow.

As the night wore on, his impatience slowly turned to frustration and he slammed his glass down on the table frequently, always making his companion jump, though she never said a word the entire evening. I was watching him at a distance of course, but I somehow felt tied to this man who walked with a cocky stride and merely had to wave his hand in order to get anything sent to him. Maybe then it dawned on me: this is who I aspired to be, a deviant, a man in control, a man with infinite vistas. I had read his books as many had in that room and I came to see the person behind the artist, a figure who remained on the periphery but was still at the centre of it, perhaps even the creator of it all. "Fuck," I thought to myself . . . Why would I want to be such a despicable character? Who logically has the want to be someone who is despised or hated? Don't we all want to be exalted in some way?

Regardless, I continued watching him as he moved closer to where the main event was to take place that night. What was going to happen was a secret, perhaps only known to a small group within that building that night . . .

As promised, close to the striking of midnight like something out of a bad horror movie, the main event began. Two men came out of the shadows: one dressed only in a pair of tight latex shorts and another who appeared to be his assistant, both stern looking and athletic. The group remained silent but surreptitiously gathered in closer, none closer than Mantra Hand himself as the assistant began by rigging up a harness attached to long steel hooks that dangled in the air over the large bulkhead. Those steel hooks seemed to win over the crowd, though the hush that followed seemed weighted with fear.

This scene, obviously foreign to me, felt as though it were stuck in slow motion. As he began taking the hooks and threading them through his Flesh, one did not have to extrapolate too much to figure out his intentions. He laid himself out flat on the floor as the dozen or so hooks hung impaled in his milky flesh, eyes closed, a murmuring coming from his lips as his assistant slowly lifted him off the ground and into the air, his body taking on the appearance of a victim of medieval torture, but that was where it all changed . . .

As he began to sway himself back and forth, an ecstasy overtook him as the surge of endorphins flowed through his veins. Any pain that he may have felt in the beginning had now been dampened by something individually pure. All the various masked and made-up faces around me looked at him in rapt awe, though I could see Mantra Hand gently twisting the hilt of his cane to reveal a blade he had concealed within. Without a word he walked out into the centre, much to everyone's surprise, and stopped the performer only to place the edge of the blade over his neck. Not a breath was taken until the crimson bloom unfurled and we were told the performance was over . . .

Blind

The harrowing experience of being an outside observer...

Without question he has a disposition that is sometimes angry and dreadfully boring and pedantic. He definitely doesn't see it, nor does he want to, due in part to his ego that seems to surface when he feels as though he is being attacked from all angles, even if it is obvious— from my standpoint at least—that people are trying to help him rather than hinder him. Sometimes he is far too sensitive about simple matters and far too detached from matters of seriousness. Does he know this? Does he want to know this? Well, it would appear to be the former rather than the latter. It's hard being his friend sometimes, but not often . . . I couldn't imagine being his lover, as I fear that he would become obsessive and quite possibly disturbed.

All in all, the meaning he seems to seek in others is really a seeking of meaning within himself. I don't think he realizes how self-referential he is in his musings when it comes to literature, music, art, or anything else for that matter, as though his interpretations are somehow more deeply meaningful than anyone else. One could call it an intellectual hubris—or in other words, a lack of intellectual honesty. I would also dare to say that he holds a pessimism close to his heart and mind and he is afraid to express it in any meaningful way. That is not to say he doesn't like to communicate feelings, but there is a shroud or secret attached to them and the true meaning of his words are often covered as well.

What else can I say? This is who he is and all he will ever be . . .

RYAN MADEJ

Open

The love of the profane, the mad, the ugly . . .
Yes, yes, but also a love of the beautiful, the
complex, the transcendent. Feeling as much as
fucking, speaking as much as listening, listening to
jazz as much as grievous math metal in the dark. It
all makes sense to me as perhaps it does to others.
No need for explanation or exposition, exegesis or
extrapolation; the formula is all there and maybe
has been the only real constant in my life, a
grounding mechanism in the midst of chaos.
Writing has also been a constant, as others can
testify, the maternal figure included. She could
hear the whirr of my electric typewriter and the
tapping of the keys, not to mention the hard slam
each time I hit return. Co-workers could see it too
on those tired Saturday mornings, scraps of paper
in my hand where I scribbled illegible notes and
ideas in a frenzy that I no longer possess. They
must remember all those times I went on about
plots and dialogues that no longer exist, meaning-
less characters, and a thousand other tidbits that
time has made irrelevant. Yes, and they must also
remember my affair with books. That is a fire that
will never go out—the truest love I have, and
perhaps will ever have, in this lifetime. Two words
forever on my lips: Library and Literature, both

unable to exist without the other, the greatest of symbiotic relationships. That is what is open, as much as anything else I suppose. The others would also be aware that I choose to travel by foot, across bridges and streets, down alleys to dead ends, through hardened paths in the valley, up stairs in unfamiliar buildings, into darkened parkades and empty lots, walking past fights and skirmishes and into the night ahead. If that isn't preferable, a train would do nicely; a World Train that connects the Continents and goes over seas and inlets, prairie and jungle, into the Unknown.

Yes, this is what is important and open . . . the means by which I write, read, and walk.

THE THRESHOLD AND THE KEY

The Man Behind the Monster

The Alchemy of Sleep

The deeper and more distressing the dream, the deeper and more distressed I feel upon waking. What happens so often in that world of dreams centres around a mosaic city, perhaps born from snippets of how I imagine cities like Prague, Buenos Aires, and Tokyo. Despite this, the backstreets, the boulevards and the tree-lined avenues feel familiar and slightly sinister in much the same way they have always felt as I've done my walking tours through Midtown. The faces have also become more familiar as years have passed, whereas at one point in time my dreams were just a series of strangers. What is distressing about these dreams is how familiar they have become by the sheer fact that they seem to be replicating my waking world. Upon waking the heaviness that slides over from the dream world takes me by surprise and for a quarter of an hour I wonder if I'm still dreaming. Oddly, this happens mostly on weekends when all is silent and undisturbed in my house and the chill of getting out of bed is just as terrible as opening my eyes. During those years in the Vayu the value of dreams was lost on me, perhaps because the innocence of youth is so dream-like in itself, for there is no demand for logic or control. Now, decades later, my mind must be searching for what has become lost.

The awareness of that other world has, quite logically I assume, belonged to the realm of the Unknown, where distinguishing between what is real and what is not can never be a central issue, for I've always come to believe that a truth lies in that world of dream, despite my better judgement. More than anything else the central image of my dreams has been the city—the city as prison, the city as hope and the city as eternal mystery. The walls of Midtown lead back to ancient cities such as Jericho and Damascus, whose very history revolves in part with that one physical aspect: the Wall. As much as a wall can be seen as symbol of protection, it can also be seen as an obstacle in one's life.

Such is the dual nature of the city and how it functions within the dream state. In one instance the landscape can appear as one of opportunity and the fantastic, with the replication of the female form like in Adolfo Bioy Casares' novel *The Invention of Morel,* or it can be a place of deception and hard luck reminiscent of Chandler's legendary Philip Marlowe whose excursions around Los Angeles usually led him to contemplate the city as a malevolent force. Either way, the outcome is similar in the sense that one feels a great weight come upon them when they visit the Dream City, through the sensual and beautiful, or the dark and bloody. One need to look only at *Invisible Cities* by Italo Calvino or the city of Celephais in Lovecraft to know these contrasts. In other words, sleep can be dangerous in that our hopes and fears are never really far from us, even when we close our eyes.

Knowing this, we still have a total dependence on sleep. It's biological, without it we would die—putting us into another kind of sleep, one of permanence and finality that, sadly, is the fate of us all. Yet we don't fear sleep like we fear death, due, I'm sure, to the temporary nature of the former and the absolute finality of the latter. I have died many deaths in my dreams as well, enough ways to feel that our existence in our waking lives may give way to many other varieties of demise when we take our final breath. That thought alone has kept me up many nights until the breaking of dawn, and perhaps that is not only the enigma of sleep, but its strange alchemy as well.

"To sleep, perchance to dream," as Hamlet famously said . . . "that undiscovered country" . . . and on and on . . . Within the walls of that old house, which still haunts the cities of my dreams to this day, I could at least feel, to some degree, a respite from the nightmares that would find me once I left its walls. Still I ache for that familiarity, and that is sad and hopeless, I know, even if it means reliving all that went on there. That is the strangeness of sleep: do we ever truly wake up?

A Feeling of Ugliness

I've always given free rein to fantasy whenever the cup of creativity has been empty. Even before I put pen to paper, a sickening need for the shadows and side streets flowed through my veins. Trying to trace a ground zero or a catalyst of some kind for these feelings and impulses has often proven difficult, almost intractable, even at the best of times. It's at times like these that I turn back to the Library, but not my own, rather that of my parents. Theirs was a library—a strange mixture of desserts made for the Devil, if that's a possibility at all. Both of my parents seemed attracted to crime, particularly the maternal figure who at one time worked in a maximum security prison. Hers was a collection of books of true crime, criminal psychology, and madness in general.

Of course, there were other books too, but those books were generally forgettable—titles like Herman Wouk's *War and Remembrance* and others of the same ilk. The father figure carved a similar path in the literary sand, reading Max Haines books or run-off from the maternal section. As a boy wandering through our home, I would see these books sitting on the edge of the bathtub or underneath end tables, even at the foot of the bed, sometimes as doorstops, their covers bent or the pages slightly water damaged. These books sometimes found their way onto the same shelves as the encyclopedias I had mentioned before, looking out of place like a corpse in the middle of a dinner party. So where did this feeling of ugliness come from? Was it from the embarrassment of my parents having a collection of books that uninspiring? Or from the fact that the material in these books was ugly in itself? Perhaps it was a bit of both. In later years I saw my parent's taste in books change, especially the maternal figure, when she returned to school and took up English Literature. Soon her bookshelf was full of the classics, all of which I might add were from a period of literary history I've had little or no interest in, authors such as Thackery, Dickens, Smollett, Sterne . . . dry novels one finds in the bargain section of used bookstores, where eventually all literature ends up after a few centuries when the memory and significance of the author is forgotten with the inevitable passage of time. Regardless, books as well as crime began to take shape in my mind in quite an unusual way. By the time I had reached my teen years my rebellion was not in committing crimes, though some of the people I was associating with at the time had certainly delved into its lower levels while I stood on the sidelines listening to their stories of mischief. No, my rebellion came from the Library itself by living vicariously through the lives of not only the characters, but the authors who created them. Much like one of my literary heroes—William S. Burroughs—who through the Library also found his liberation and an early desire to write, I too found something similar in his writings . . . a breaking through . . . a door . . . a Threshold, which was one of many. The same could be said of the work of Louis-Ferdinand Céline, Albert Camus, or Jean Genet. When I sit back and think about it, I owe much to the French literary world and their constant desire to change how we view the novel, and their unabashed views on nearly everything. Perhaps I felt like a literary criminal back then, not knowing the dangers of letting my mind and emotions loose because of books, for in all honesty it felt as though my growing obsessions were given validation by the very books that I was reading and the material within them was the kindling for a slowly growing fire that has yet to go out.

Maybe the ugliness I've felt all these years has little to do with the fact that my parents read less than reputable books; maybe it has more to do with the fact that through all those thousands of pages that have slipped anxiously through my fingers, I uncovered a wealth of material within myself that in some way feels ugly, for as Kafka so aptly put it: "a book should be an axe to break the frozen sea inside us." That frozen sea then is where this ugliness first reared its head, and Kafka too is partly to blame, but this feeling of ugliness is not true ugliness . . . No, really it's my inheritance and my wealth and I should recognize it as such and nothing more.

Fragments and a Cracked Mirror

Across the High Gate Bridge is a life that I wanted at one point, but perhaps no longer. A life full of wandering and sipping tea along the wide open streets at night, searching out books or caressing their spines in the Observatory Library. It's in the darkness or the fog, or under a full moon, that I've felt closest to God, and during a thin slice of time I felt like I knew Him better, usually when I crossed the Velox and left the centre of Midtown behind. Only in silence or beneath a deluge of lunar rays have I felt what some call 'grace.' In the daylight all is visible and of course we all know God isn't visible, so give me the night instead. Then there are people and books and the effect they both have on the psyche of those who read them. Yes, I mean reading books *and* people. I used to put my faith, much like I have in the idea of God, in people, but for a good portion of my life now I believe and put my faith in literature because books have disappointed me far less than people have. God, or the idea of God, intrigues me still so it never disappoints. On the flipside of all this is disappointing others, which I'm sure I have done, but for the time being will remain shrouded in a soundless state. . . .

Like Borges, even before I read his pages, I had

an obsession with mirrors, and like the Argentine master they mesmerized me with their infinitude. But besides the inherent metaphysical implications of the mirror there was the idea of reflection and it was standing in front of them that I began to see a crack in my personality. The push and pull of the two Fishes of my astrological sign had without any conscious prodding begun to actualize, letting the shadow emerge. "I don't remember 1989," as Matthew Good once sang, and the only real situations I can recall with any real clarity are standing in front of the mirror and the fall of the Berlin Wall, yet I knew nothing of the significance of that event. It would take nearly another decade before that happened when I began to read about Karl Marx, Communism, and nuclear weapons.

I had also read Solzhenitsyn's *Gulag Archipelago* and felt, perhaps for the first time in my short life, a genuine despair for humanity. In many ways, all I had was a faith in God and in Literature, and a belief in both is a double-edged sword. My own belief in God took a turn after the likes of Camus' *The Stranger*, *The Fall*, and *The Myth of Sisyphus* seeped into my bones and rattled my spirit. The world suddenly seemed a lot more desolate, while simultaneously becoming more beautiful and intricate, though to be honest my belief in a silent God did not leave me. I never believed God intervened in matters, but being the First Writer He continued to pen a vast masterpiece that only He could possibly understand.

The pull of the Library changed my views of God and myself, and the more I read the more I felt immune to the plagues of the world . . . or so I led myself to believe. This all changed once the first taste of Flesh fell upon my lips, as one might expect. All too often the plague and cure of one's spirit can be traced back to the sensual as the previous pages may have expressed, yet in the midst of all the confusion I felt about sexuality or the sometimes necessary importance it takes has proven to be just as inexhaustible a subject as the Library itself. As Roberto Bolaño put it—that demon of a writer who proved to me that literature is still alive —"Books are finite, sexual encounters are finite, but the desire to read and to fuck is infinite; it surpasses our own deaths, our fears, our hopes for peace." As a writer, and perhaps more importantly as a reader, the idea of profound sexual encounters takes on a kind of myth like the best of Literature does, maybe even in the same way as Nabokov described the idea of a major writer above. Three components may make up the perfect sexual encounter too, though like the rarest of books that have a profound impact on the reader, those encounters are few and far between, unless one is very discriminating and patient instead of hoping for the best.

I find it nearly impossible to tie memory to all these experiences — sex, God, books, history — in the sense that I've felt fragments of one in the other but perhaps not all at the same time. Only in a perfect world could this be possible, or at least in a world that allowed profound experimentation without judgement or ridicule. Bolaño also said something to the effect that books can feel like sex, but then he stated that this is a special and rare experience. Have I ever felt this, I ask myself?

I assume that a book of that calibre would be one that *seduces*, not necessarily through the means of sexual description or innuendo, but through the cadence and structure of the work itself. Oddly enough, the works of Burroughs and say, Kathy Acker, the female equivalent of Burroughs, have a certain seductive charm but perhaps only through the perversion and violence of the stories themselves, thus giving them the designation of 'transgressive.' The hanging and orgasmic deaths that seem to run rampant in Burroughs' early work from *Naked Lunch* to *Nova Express* brought out a primordial essence when I read them, the dual forces of Eros and Thanatos Freud was so hung up on in his own research into the mind. Acker, whose *Empire of the Senseless* serves as the Anima to those Burroughs novels, did something similar, but that book can hardly be described as erotic, at least in any conventional sense, which might be the point. Regardless, when it came to the works of Mantra Hand and the mystery that surrounded him and his works, I felt I came to know something Others didn't, not only in him, but in myself. A burden had begun to lift thanks to writers likes them, but no, I couldn't say I felt seduced by them . . . rather, liberated in some sense. One thing is certain about those works just mentioned: God truly does not exist in those universes, meaning I cannot in good conscience say they are perfect works, though the memory of a time in my life where I really questioned the existence of a God made each of them a perfect work, an antidote to a poison that had infected my body and mind.

Somewhere along the way, my literary tastes had begun to broaden and the sexual tensions began to ease. For better or worse, the mask began to loosen and from the well of the infinite Library came not only books, but also the emergence of some deep-seated desires that had never had an opportunity to be played out in the real world . . .

I recall Georges Bataille's *Story of the Eye* being a book that stirred those strange, erotic waves. Often it is not the material represented or the coital acts displayed, or even the style by which an author writes something, but rather the *transgressive act* itself that provides a deep inspiration to create, whether it be on the page or in the bedroom. Though I've never read the works of the Marquis de Sade, from my own subjective vantage point based on what I've heard and read about the man, he created a life so completely attuned to his erotic whims that he was able to translate those acts into infamous works of literature, becoming something of a legend in the process.

What has history done to these ideas of sex, violence, and the like? Have we been freed from the chains of our own minds when it comes to these subjects? I've asked myself this question many times after closing many books and have no clear answer, but I will say this, if I may: regardless of the book at hand and the subject matter contained therein, the purpose of literature stays the same, whether it intends to or not. The purpose is to *disturb* the equilibrium of the reader; in other words, to throw the order of one's mental, physical, and spiritual being into chaos. That is what literature continues to do to me and to everyone who takes the matter seriously: it takes us apart and scatters us to the wind, and just when we think we've pieced ourselves back together, it happens all over again. There may be nothing so joyous . . .

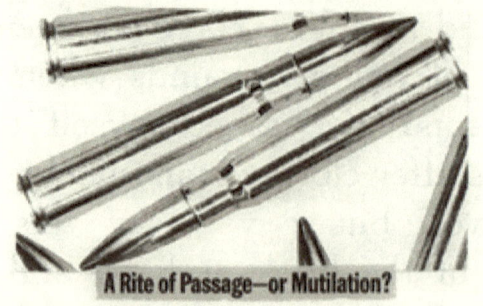

A Rite of Passage—or Mutilation?

The Best Places to Die

Again, and perhaps always, I return to the house, its strange aura, and the nostalgic grip that continues to slowly strangle me with old memories. One memory is poignant, however, since few experiences have had such a lasting effect on me. The year is uncertain, but I know the gears of spring had begun to turn while the lingering symptoms of a flu flowed through my body. For some reason I spent the day alone wrapped in blankets, sipping ginger ale, watching mindless television and vomiting. Somewhere in the back of my mind—irrationally, as one thinks when they feel very ill—was a desire to die. Everything around me pulsed with a deep silence. I had turned the volume down on the television and my attention was drawn toward the window where the virgin rays of sunlight came flooding in through the dirty glass. The scene was idyllic for a perfect death and my young mind welcomed it. There was no fear or anxiety, only the idea of peace. It was an entirely pure experience that I have never forgotten and I have chased that sense of peace ever since, coming no closer to its recapture.

Inevitably, with the passing years and the dark pall that surrounds death here in the West—the

West itself being a symbol of death—my own thoughts about the subject began to darken as well, but more than that I began to dwell on ideal locations to greet death in order to recapture that sense of peace. It may have started when I read Dostoyevsky in my teens and learned that he had died on a couch after suffering a stroke, an ending I envied because I had been in a similar place and I feel that if my life had ended in that moment I would have been okay with a comfortable closing of the curtain, rather than dying in the sterilized prison of a hospital.

By the time I picked up the works of Yukio Mishima, a man who committed ritual seppuku at his physical and creative peak, a need to perish outside the societal norm had almost become a priority, an obsession. Suicide didn't cease to be an option for years to come since other Japanese literary heroes of mine also took their own lives: Ryūnosuke Akutagawa and Yasunari Kawabata. Suicide in the land of the rising sun doesn't have the same negative stigma and connotations that we attach to it here and this is obvious in the great historical example of the samurai, who at the pinnacle of honour and service felt it would be disgraceful not to follow one's master into death. The *Hagakure or Book of the Samurai*, a book praised and valued by Mishima, lays the foundation for right conduct and condones this action.

To die on a battlefield is a much written about situation that bears very little resemblance to what I would call an ideal death, though I can imagine myself on my back, a fatal wound in my belly, staring up at a cloudless sky as the coup de grâce is brought down by my enemy. Beyond that scene lies a series of other locations where I tend to see myself. Sadly, some of those scenes lead me back to the Western Quarter, and perhaps even more pathetically, back to the house itself. Somewhere among those intrepid thoughts are the real fantasies, the real desires, where I hope death awaits me.

The Window

I imagine a particular window, incredibly large in fact, with a thick frame, that stretches into infinity, where I can lay down in silence and cast my gaze upon a calm, blue sea with the sun just over the horizon, my last breath fogging the glass. A slightly warm breeze enters from the same window and the smell of sea salt and the sounds of gulls upon the water reach my ears and nose as the air leaves my lungs forever. Is it wrong to contemplate this finale? Perhaps . . . Curiosity and morbidity seem to go hand-in-hand to some degree and I always seem to seek them; however, in this instance my fantasy has next to nothing to do with morbidity and more to do with one's perception of the future, no matter how unlikely it may be . . .

The Cocoon
(A Ritual)

In light of an Ending, if it is foreseeable, one must somehow ground themselves and prepare in a manner that departs from the norm. I say this as though it were easy, perhaps even necessary, but the fact remains: how are you going to react at the End? Mishima, whose violent ending seemed grotesquely appropriate for the kind of man he was, spent years playing out his own death in film and in his own works, culminating in a final coup de grâce provided by one of the members of his private army. Of course we shouldn't all go to these extremes, but as our births into this world are documented as great events, shouldn't our endings be as well?

From this thought comes the idea of the cocoon, where the warmest of blankets is wrapped around me, my head protruding slightly, and the weight of the world begins to lift off of me as if by magic. Yes, the cocoon is symbolic, not just of rebirth but of a transformation that we are all forced into whether we like it or not, whether we are brave or cowardly. Perhaps this idea first came to me when I saw a photo of the great philosopher Ludwig Wittgenstein, who in his final moments lay wrapped in blankets in much the same fashion. It also comes down to a matter of comfort as it all begins to fall away, disappearing forever.

The Back Alley

There is always a certain romanticism to my thoughts in regards to my demise. I believe, perhaps irrationally, that these elevated thoughts will somehow make the transition into the nether-world easier. What I don't consider in all of this is the very real possibility of never fulfilling any of these wishes and that, like most people, I will get the end I deserve, not the one I want. In other words, at least in this instance, death will imitate life. Regardless, the thoughts continue unabated and fall back into the realm of fantasy, that tried and true place where I find myself most of the time, avoiding reality like one might avoid the plague.

Raymond Chandler might be to blame, as I take no responsibility as a writer for the outside influences that guide me. Rather, I absorb them like a sponge and spit them out in the most subversive way I can. Thank you, Mr. Chandler, wherever you are. Anyway, yes, he might be to blame, much in the same way as my parents and their reading material: through the lens of crime. Chandler's Philip Marlowe stands as the prototype of a cool, intelligent detective with a chip on his shoulder. His perambulations around Los Angeles at a time in history where everything seemed cooler makes a death in a back alley seem all the more enticing. Of course, in situations such as these the setting must be perfect: darkened, rain-soaked evening under the hush of a dimming streetlamp, an obscured killer in the distance holding a revolver, the trail of blood mixing with the fallen rain that ends up draining into a nearby sewer. The only smells that remain in those final moments are those of the fresh ozone and the gunpowder, a sweet aroma that brings together the essence of life and death. The difficulty of living, at least at this point of my life, is trying to separate myself from Art. Not because I want to, but in the inevitable End I don't want to weep over it like I would a person I love. That being said, I probably will anyway.

The Desert

The desert has brought us many interesting stories throughout the centuries, from the tame to the grotesque. Aleister Crowley, in 1909, set out into the desert on his way to Algiers with a faithful male lover to face the Demon Choronzon in a ritual of magic and drugs (according to legend or truth—depending on the source—whether it be Crowley himself or the academics). It was also out in the desert, in 1904, in the chamber of the Great Pyramid, that Crowley began his true ascent as a mage when he conducted the Bornless Ritual of the Ars Goetia and within days had *The Book of the Law* dictated to him by the entity known as Aiwass. Whether one wants to believe it or not, the desert is a spiritual place where founders of other faiths—besides the infamous founder of Thelema—went to contact entities, and also a place where they, like Crowley, encountered the dark forces of the Universe and perhaps the subsequent madness that accompanies contact with said forces. Within the strange beauty of the sand, the sky and the emptiness that they exude seems like the ideal place to lay down my bones . . . to be able to rest my body up against a rock, my lips chapped from the intense heat, my brow pouring with sweat as the vultures and creatures living in deep crevices come out to play with my flesh. Perhaps I can also envision the desert as a location for my own final ritual, where the forces that have guided my life finally come to me in a staggering display as my eyes begin to close for the last time. That grand place where it seems life and death always come close enough together to shake hands and divide up the spoils . . . Or maybe I just fantasize and wish for too much.

(I)

The Threshold
(Apotheosis)

"I'm in you now"

An empty street, the LEDs of late night contemplation flashing above me . . . It's the end of the cycle once more. I've reached the summit of my desires. I just kept on denying it as I looked at the cobra head on the hilt of my sword cane. *Snap out of it, quit torturing yourself with this euphoric business.* A sense of an ending, over and over, played out before my mind's eye in a test pattern. My behaviour had been somewhat erratic and I wanted to bury the past in a shallow plot just in case I wanted to dig it up again in the future, which I always seemed to do in times of desperation. Images of me as a senile old man got loud as fuck and a desperation came over me as the night melted . . .

Dismantled, shattered, no real modus operandi to guide me other than my phallus.

She had covered herself in a thin white robe. The room was small and the house was old, the neighbourhood familiar from years of riding in car at the same time of night, looking at the father figure's profile. I remember thinking of doves and asteroids, my limbs heavy as lead, hoping the call of her flesh would be the magic midnight powder that I needed. A swarming crescendo moved through me as she bit her lip and smiled, and revealed more of her white stockinged legs.

-Did you know that a woman was murdered here and that they never found the body?

She said this as she massaged my back with her warm fingers. The breath of the moment turned to deep kisses before I could say much more and her presence fogged my mind/body. If it were true it couldn't have been more appropriate to be there, to the hilt of the hill, upon the ghost of a body slain and disappeared. Her dark hair moved over my chest and her teeth hit mine in a frenzy of wet tongues.

Golden horses galloped through my thoughts as her face vanished between my legs. I could hear the television and possible narcs across the street in the empty winter night.

Her face in the morgue split across my vision like a dive bomb . . .

-I'm a bad person, I thought . . . a fucking pig . . . a slave to instinct, or just a slave . . . unwell, fucked up, being chased by piranhas . . . ready to face the Void. I heard her soft moans as she downed another vial, slurring herself into a chemically induced oblivion. I lifted her onto me and a natural cruelty came over me in a hot-headed fashion . . . For a few moments at least, any thoughts of a self-inflicted wound to the body left my mind and put me into a catatonic jungle where the strangest of animals played, the two of us being a couple of them, full of good ideas soon to be well executed on the other.

My nerves unravelled following her comment about the dead woman, which struck me with a mausoleum treatment. Her words were my remedy and served to settle something in my mind, and an arc of doves skipped across my grey matter in a matter of seconds before disappearing . . . Yes, the Mysterious Threshold. How did I know? I only came to realize it when I saw her tattoo which covered the area just above her collarbone by her right shoulder . . . a Key fashioned in an old style . . . a Key that would unlock anything, a Skeleton Key of Eros and Thanatos embedded on this liquid young woman who fucked people in the Land of the Dead and left them disjointed.

I was one of the disjointed ones. The kind who wanted to hear the crack of a whip and see the advancement and destruction of pawns. The kind who would want to see Houdini escape from the Void itself and proclaim himself God. She gave me all that without me even begging, it was as if Fate somehow existed for the smallest of moments in order to give me something I needed through the body of a young woman who talked about murder during sex.

My chrome carcass seemed to shake to her music and all I could imagine with my mind's eye was a sorrowful chain of events that felt off-planet. Her hands and body above me caused a strange turbulence to take place where we seemed to merge and the lights in the room began to dim ... an invasive kind of feeling where the outer rim of reality is touched by the Unknown and you're not sure if you will make it back again. She became a silhouette in the astral ritual I had created months before, a nomad who was waiting for only me at the final exit in silence, ten thousand leagues below the surface of my feelings.

Afterward we shared some good green magic through the glass pipe and chatted nonchalantly about previous wars and endangered species, the reason being that she had been watching a show about animals just before I arrived and I thought that the rest of us were not long for this planet either, whether we knew it or not. We talked about Agent Orange and the tragic demise of Sherlock Holmes at the hands of Moriarty, only to be brought back to life shortly thereafter by Conan Doyle.

-Only in literature is resurrection possible and

hopefully immortality, I said quietly.

She didn't hear me but smiled nonetheless. I couldn't keep my eyes off her tattoo which told me I had completed my goal . . . she took notice of my line of vision and laughed, running her fingers over the Key.

-You want to know why I got this?

-Sure, tell me.

She thought about it for a moment before looking back at me with bloodshot eyes.

-Because there is always a new door to be unlocked.

What a tiny fox in the making, I thought . . . Why is it always woodland animals?

Her hands caressed a silver rubber dildo before throwing it on the ground and grimacing. Outside, a low humming sound tickled the air before disappearing, and I could still taste her flesh in my saliva. She talked briefly about the lowlands to the South where she was from and I tried to imagine how life really was outside the Wall.

-Yes, there is always a new door to be unlocked.

-Of course there is . . . that's what keeps my pussy wet. The notion that there is always more to be found whether it is good or bad, beautiful or ugly, stupid or profound. Only assholes don't care enough to explore anything in any great detail . . .

Am I right?

-Yes. Most definitely.

In the space of the brief silence that followed, a wave of uncertainty seemed to fall on top of me like a piece of dark sapphire. I had made massive demands on this woman who I barely knew and like so many she wouldn't be a part of my life for long, but that was okay . . . she had given me the Key, a passcode to move on to the next phase, a knife with which to metaphorically slit my throat, a new soul, a new level of speaking.

It was very late when I stepped outside into the winter night heavy with that typical murderous silence. We parted with a quick kiss and I took one last look at the Key before walking through the deserted streets. I felt gleefully traumatized, my head full with riptides and sense of "fuck the world" moving along my spine. No doubts followed me and for once in a long while I felt okay with myself. My mind had burst so fully that the cigarette in my hand nearly burned my fingers, a result of my lack of interest . . .

(II)

"It's not the potion, it's the magic that I seek"
                              - Annie Clark (St. Vincent)

All too often, beyond the fantasies of ideal deaths and ideal places, are the real problems that arise from the expansion of consciousness, that of the actual noose one may make—either literally or metaphorically. Many times the playfulness that comes from contemplating suicide in any real way has had me questioning my own sanity. It is a comforting thought though, as Nietzsche pointed out in *Beyond Good and Evil* and yes, it has gotten me through many a bad night and many a bad day as well. To return to the house one final time might liberate me from this type of thinking, but even that could probably not repair what has already been done: setting me on the road through the Unknown. The people that have accompanied me on this journey, whether willingly or not, have not realized how much of an asset they have been, and it is perhaps due to their proximity to me that has not allowed them to come to this conclusion as well.

Despite this, I offer a second prayer . . .

Ata yigdal na koach Ado-nai

"Now, I pray, let the Power of God be Great"

The more I contemplate, the more the mental disease rises but at the same time gives me clarity in a time of confusion. From this clarity comes amor fati (the love of one's fate) and the embracing of this concept. Amen indeed. Those who have followed are the magic, the secret ingredient, the chosen ones who through the mystery of the Universe helped guide me through, and hopefully I did the same. You are all the source of my joy, my chaos, my desire to stave off the noose. I owe you all too much, but I thank you anyway . . .

"Maakaral Shivaya Namaha"

(III)

Across an Opaque Sky

The Shaman has yet to appear. I await them as I disconnect, Maya always at play in the background. Yes, the play of Illusion. I know how I was conceived: up the sleeve of a fuck-up who paid no mind to what was and what is. Pay it no mind, I tell myself, it's illogical to go on thinking that a definitive transformation won't come or that I won't snatch it from the sky itself. There is a life beyond all the fetishes and obsessions, bad memories and insomniac nights, the lifeless kisses and empty banter coming from the streets below. The past will eventually disown me and the future will cradle me and all those terrible experiences will dissolve. That is Maya. That is illusion. That is what I continue to see in the rearview as I pull away from the curb and drive into the arms of the night I love so much.

There were points of escape and if it had been possible back then to see the many errors I had made, perhaps the end result would have been different . . . meaning I could have found peace on an island and quickly forgotten the world. When I first began to meditate in my teens I had an experience I have not and probably will never forget, when I went so deeply into my mind I could no longer feel my body, all the while sensing that I was going back in time to the Beginning, the Alpha, where all matter originated . . . Though as my mind began to pull away, something deep within me said 'no' and I have never been able to recover that feeling in all the years since. Was that the verge of enlightenment? Maybe, maybe not. Whatever it was, I've longed for it ever since and only caught glimpses of it through various lenses and shifts in perception, feeling the grip of reality tighten around me more as I try to embrace the Unknown one more time.

(IV)

Forging a Skeleton Key

The Key, forged out of the idea of the Flesh, finds its endpoint across the Threshold. An intense light rushes out and the cockroaches of the mind go scurrying back into the darkness that bred them in the first place. How often had I departed in the middle of the night to follow my own shadow? In my most lucid moments I see three scenes: the tree-lined streets of the Vayu where the House still stands and the memories linger in weightless anticipation of my return which will never happen, the path that slices through the heart of Midtown that so few notice and even fewer walk, never taking in the sights and sounds which are nondescript and silent—in other words, perfect—and finally the Square where I spent so much time alone under the threat of rain or snow, reading or sketching out my desires on lined pages.

Write slowly. Read slowly. Let the light back in . . . let the blind lead those who can see but can't feel, as a wise man once alluded to through music. Let go of the threats and anxieties that well up from the Abyss. Cross it and face the Demon. Recite the words and leave the Ego behind, become weightless and determined. This is the real challenge and the real goal, isn't it my friends? But how difficult is it to leave the massive forces of Eros and Thanatos behind to search further? Difficult indeed. One still needs to feed the serpent . . .

(V)

Baptism by Fire

The pleasant throbbing of an unreal blindness brought on by endless days in the Vayu lounges. Roughly speaking, I had been living two lives: one of honest searching and another of honest self-absorption/destruction. Both lives seemed like viable options as the sun's last rays drifted over my shoulders, turning away from the desk where the automatic hand scribbled and the empty bottles lay. I had imagined a life where the end equalled the beginning: lonely but free. In these daydreams I smoked cigarettes by the sea and watched the city under the fog, waiting for winter to end. A person more than feels loneliness, it penetrates to the very depth of one's mind and body, eventually poisoning the spirit. In those weak but tense moments is when one truly begins to awaken, however, and the actions taken in those moments become a reflection of who you really are . . .

My hands began to explore more . . . not just my own body but the body of others . . . The Flesh . . . I spoke louder and longer . . . I departed more often and left no address, but you could often find me by the waters or sitting below the Wall . . . the Moon seemed brighter and the Sun more dull . . . Yes, the nights felt so much warmer and the days cold and empty by comparison. One of my lowest times, but also one of the most fantastic. Loosening one's grip on reality can do wonders as much as it can create a mountain of anguish. Twilight of red and gold, and over the High Gate where so many people jumped is one of the quietest places. Peering into the waters one can sometimes see the reflections of the dead and I often wondered if I would soon be joining them . . .

(VI)

Red Rose Filling the Skull

The morning sun, familiar and warm—almost contagious—ready to be eaten and easily digested. Sun eater. A blend of reddish light under The Heliotropic Cycle . . . smoke and ash. I gave myself over, trying to rebuild the House in my mind. I should have bought a gun to kill all my hopes and dreams in a solitary place away from the strangely morphing shadows . . .

. . . 2000, month and day unknown

The millennium came in almost soundlessly and the only other form of expression that I could use at the time other than writing was the spliced tapes . . . Yes, these were worthy of a type of art, but also of a crime that I may or may not have committed . . . the limbs of various ideas hung in a mental net, self-contained, deciphering my mind map, eventually comprehending it. Then came an early November wind . . . at least I think it was November . . . it probably was, considering I was in the midst of a deeply depressive state. In situations like these the mind becomes a highly complex mess of ideas and emotions, trying desperately to disentangle itself from the binary code it was infused with at birth. The effect of this disentanglement is what led to all these books in the first place . . . I might even go so far as to say that it was the process of disentanglement that gave birth to Mantra Hand himself.

It's a well known fact by now that Mr. Hand is a rather dark spirited entity/man who manifested himself subtly through the unravelling I just spoke of, but what one may not realize is that perhaps he was there from the beginning . . .

Once more we come closer to the end of the cycle where all the previous experiences and the dead weight of time somehow seem to vanish while creating a space where everything is born anew. Somewhere in the midst of this transition is where all the blood and liquid seemed to pool . . . I can't say with a straight face that I have come out of all these experiences unscathed. Wiser perhaps, but not unscathed, because there are still more memories of brutal acts that are well documented elsewhere and perhaps will see the light of day once Mantra Hand rears his ugly head once more out of the abyss and becomes that creature of unimaginable power and seduction. Seduction is the Key word here, as it always tends to be in these situations. He appears naturally with as much vanity and imperfection as any being, but he tends to speak in riddles, sometimes even backwards, always sceptical—constantly looking into the Abyss or, if the mood suits him, walking into it without looking back. The result he is looking for is to aid the Body by seeking the Flesh of Others in order to give rise to what lies outside himself. He finds this task necessary in order to find some sort of 'truth' reflected to him in dreams, causing him to delve into mathematics and algorithms in his waking moments by focusing on the following repeating numbers: 11:11, 222, 333,

444, 777, 12:12, 10:10, etc., along with a host of other synchronicities and personal numbers. Incidentally, his personal numbers correspond perfectly with my own, which cannot be coincidence. My own task of passing over the Threshold is somehow dependent upon my strength and direction at this crucial stage of writing, for it completes the Great Work I set out years ago to complete. I never would have guessed that my completion of this task would have been so personally profound, but yes, it has . . . I owe much to Mantra Hand in his present manifestation of Daath. Through him I have learned to write my history backwards only to have it mutate on the way forward. Mantra Hand's competence lies in his subtlety and his worth in the many underhanded games he has played thus far at my expense.

It is said somewhere: "Through the Formula of the Great Work his Karma gains strength and a suitable direction." This is what Mantra Hand has given me all these years. Though many times he stayed on the periphery, out of sight and out of mind, I could no doubt feel his presence, even if that meant lowering myself to certain levels of depravity. In saying that, I also gained *insight* . . . a word that seems so foreign to many people in regards to themselves; a word that through the experiences of the Smoke, the Library, the Flesh gave me access to the Threshold and ultimately the Unknown. So what will become of him now as the tide waters recede and the wind has calmed? Will he disappear back into the shadows and warm himself by the fires of Time, waiting for the right moment to burst out from the earth once more? That remains to be seen . . .

Om Namah Shivaya
(The Closing Ritual)

The Divine Milk has come forth into a realm of light, bright and pure. A hundred salutations must be placed upon Mantra Hand who has appeared to guide me to this place of rest and, hopefully, healing. I am the progeny of his appearance and a product of his strange beauty. His presence, whether wanted or not, was needed. I collapsed into his arms and embraced the First Method of Attainment he set forth. I can see beauty now in the winters past and the sorrow in the summers we walked through together. Can I assume that my mind has found strength and that my wanderings in the wilderness have produced sweet fruit? Yes, I can say that without question. Perhaps now is the time to sing hymns and to prepare the mind, to walk amongst the clouds with a new force, to ascend into the infinite armed with the light of the Moon and Sun. The end of a cycle brings with it a chance to begin anew; a chance to step up to the Altar of Experience and sacrifice another lamb and to bathe in its blood for a while as the Sea remains calm and the sky is clear.

I need rest because I have exceeded what I set out to do from the start, even though I have slept with serpents and spiders, devourers of wealth, and watched for the assassin's bullet. Maybe I feared the bullet would come from myself? Don't fear others, always fear yourself. As I write these final pages spring is in the air again, ready for the taking. The haze that has so often hung over me has begun to lift and the horizon, though full of black clouds, is full of promise. The Flesh lays behind me now and the Library in front of me with its thousands of pages spread out like a treasure map, waiting to be dissected. I used to tremble before the Light and walk bravely into the Dark, but I can see a reversal happening and it is written upon the page like this . . .

The Universe, the Abyss in perfect satisfaction.
Solve et Coagula.

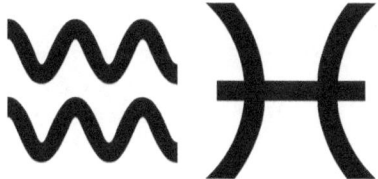